Fighting for it

USA TODAY BESTSELLING AUTHOR

ALLYSON LINDT

To every geek girl,
everywhere,
own your wierdness.

Chapter One

Anyone who said network installation wasn't sexy, never had the right scenery. And when it came to great views, it didn't get much better than Cole Denton, AKA Oz. As in The Wizard of.

Watching him lay cable—not a euphemism—along the bases of cubicles, so it could be connected and then hidden, was a thing of beauty. The way his back muscles flexed under his T-shirt… The deftness of his fingers as he crimped twisted pair… Wowza.

I was such a freaking dork. And proud of it. Best part was, Oz was too. Back in the day, he was top brass at Rinslet, one of the biggest gaming companies in the world. It was where he got the nickname, Oz. He preferred to be the man behind the curtain, making the magic happen.

He retired at thirty-five, and now, two years later, he'd founded an organization that offered tech apprenticeships.

"I was scanning the list of EdgeBite contestants this morning." I snapped another cubicle panel in place to hide wires. I preferred programming over manual labor, so I watched all the innovations, amateur or corporate, so I could dive into the tech as soon as the opportunity presented itself. "That they have a think tank out of Silicon Valley this year— Is that redundant, aren't they all?"

"No. They're just noisiest about it." Oz's tone was flat.

"Okay." I didn't mind the gruffness. He was one of those guys who was like that. I expected to carry most of this conversation, which I hated with strangers, but it was okay with Oz. "Anyway, one of competing companies has a new rendering algorithm that extrapolates from video and makes digital characters look real. Like, closer than we've ever been to the other side of the uncanny valley." The previews of their 3D models were *amazing*.

Oz moved a ladder under an open ceiling panel. "Up."

I climbed into the hole, leaned over to grab the bundle of cables from him, and headed for the next pillar to connect these. The first time he had me do this today, I'd teased him that he only picked me for the job because I was tiny and better at crawling through walls.

He'd given me a completely flat expression and said *Busted*. Anyone else would've thought he was serious, but I knew he was teasing me.

In my fantasies, his teasing took a much more physical form. He was still quiet in my imagination.

Rough, intense, and working my body over with those skilled fingers, until I was sore and pleasantly spent. Then cuddling after.

Not that I ever expected that to happen in real life. He was a decade older than me, my mentor, and basically a tech god. I was a chatty, sunshiny noob to him, and I was fine with that.

"No comment?" I called down as I worked.

"They built the tech so they could make more realistic porn."

I grinned. These were the conversations I lived for with Oz. He had perspectives I'd never consider, and while they weren't always the most positive—okay, they really never were—I learned so much about the industry this way. "You assume. Besides, the internet is so vast thanks to porn."

Silence again.

I poked my head through the nearest opening in the ceiling tile. "No comment?"

"I'm your boss. I'm not talking porn with you."

When he offered to personally work with me as part of his company's program, to give me next level training, I almost died. Mr. Smart, Sexy-as-all-get-out, was going to teach me new tricks, and make sure I didn't violate my probation in the process.

Wiring an office for CAT6 wasn't supposed to be on the lesson list, I knew this stuff, but there was a scheduling conflict and he'd offered me an extra five hundred bucks to help. I would've done it for free, but I couldn't afford to turn that down.

"You're my *mentor*, and I'm not asking about porn. I'm asking about the tech. They could've made it for other reasons."

"They could've, but they didn't. They pitched an investor friend. Disgusting pitch." Oz knew so many people in the industry.

I was both intrigued by his statement and wasn't going to ask for more detail. His definition of disgusting could be actually disgusting, in which case I'd rather not hear. If he was talking about a little kink, I'd still rather not hear. Best not to destroy the fantasy.

"Even if they did create it for that, it can be used for other things. Video games are only the start." Though they were what I was most interested in. I *super* was lucky that my best friend's previously ex-, now current-again-boyfriend had pulled some strings with my felony conviction. Gotten me a reduced sentence. Made sure I wasn't completely cut off from technology, especially not the way my *accomplice* was. But game programming and security was where I really wanted to be, and that had been out of my reach for the last couple of years.

The good news was I'd finished my probation a few months ago. My felony had been reduced to a

fighting for it

misdemeanor. I'd be re-entering the industry in no time.

Oz's sigh carried the heavy weight of *why do you have to be so damn optimistic?* "3D renders that pass for real could put people out of work with training videos, digital tellers—"

"Any tech can put people out of work." I scooted to the edge of the nearby opening in the ceiling, grabbed the lip, and dropped down the few feet to the ground, rather than using the ladder. I was short, and I was nimble. "It can also create jobs. You can put the programming behind one of these to do training videos in places where there's no Cole Denton to offer apprenticeships for hands-on work. Or as an avatar for someone who's uncomfortable with their appearance for whatever reason. There's as much potential for good as for porn."

"This is why you'd make a shitty super villain." Oz's tone was flat, but amusement flashed in his eyes.

"I really would be bad at it. Why? Are you looking for a second?"

He raised an eyebrow. "Are you saying I *would* make a good super villain?"

I shrugged. Wiring was done except for the clean-up, but I wouldn't be the one to point out we could call it a day. "If the shoe fits…" And wowza they were big shoes. Was it true what *they* said about shoe size? "Think about it. The brooding tech genius who used to work for two of the city's best-known billionaires."

"Who left of my own volition. I don't have any issues with them."

"Exactly." I was making my point, and pleased.

Oz looked at me, waiting for me to expand on what he thought was a ridiculous reply.

I didn't have to hear the words; I saw it in his blank stare. "It's always the ones people don't expect," I said. *Duh.*

Oz shook his head in disgust. "In that case, what's my deal? If I'm a super villain, what do I want? Certainly not world domination."

"Um… vengeance." I should have worked harder on motive before making my declaration.

"For what?"

"For anyone who has the intelligence to create tech to change the world, but uses their powers to take advantage of others." Like the people who used me. Who set me up to take the fall for their plan. I shook the unpleasant thought aside.

"Like the people who used you." Oz being in my head was more comforting than creepy. "That makes me the good guy."

It really did, but I was making a point. "All villains think they're in the right."

fighting for it

The corner of his mouth tugged up. If he wasn't careful, he might smile. "If I were what you say, a genius mastermind super villain, I'd pick you as my second. Without question."

Was that a catch in his voice? My phone chimed before I could process. "Sorry. I forgot to silence it." One of Oz's rules was no phones on the job. I didn't usually have an issue with it, because Violet was the only person who called me, and she didn't tend to do so during business hours. I grabbed my phone, and the name *Graham* caught my eye. My pulse kicked up, and I hesitated over the alert. Now wasn't the time to read it.

"Luna?" Oz sounded concerned.

I shook my head, set the phone to quiet, and pocketed it. "Sorry."

"Don't worry about it, we're done anyway. You look like you've seen a ghost."

In a way I had. In college, Graham was my computer science professor. He taught me so much. He was also, as far as the law was concerned, my accomplice in the hack that made us both felons. That was one bit of probation that pulling strings didn't get me around—I wasn't allowed to associate with Graham. No one cared that a few years after the law-breaking piece of code, before we were busted, we'd written another virus cleaner that stopped a massive piece of ransomware.

Did I completely lust after Graham? Yeah, but our relationship hadn't been like that. Did I have a thing for older men who were willing to share the secrets of the universe with me? Apparently.

Would I act on it? No. Sexy daydreams were nice, but knowledge was orgasmic. I'd started a search program to find him the instant I was legally allowed, so I could say *hi*. No other reason.

It also didn't escape me that I had an Oz in my life, just like my very favorite ever fictional redhead. Biggest differences between Willow Rosenberg and me? My college girlfriend almost landed me in prison, and if I was going to rock a corset, it would be microfiber, not leather.

"Luna?" Oz prodded again.

Right. "I know where Graham is."

"Hmm."

I expected that. *Everyone* in tech knew the sensationalized version of my story. Or they had. So glad that memory was fading for the public. Oz knew more of the details, but he didn't believe that Graham had nothing to do with setting me up, or sucking me into the scheme to begin with.

It had all been me. I couldn't resist the challenge, and when I asked for his help, never telling him what it was for, he'd helped.

I was to blame, and I owed Graham an apology for squashing his career.

fighting for it

My fingers twitched by my side, wanting to grab my phone. Work was over. I could excuse myself and go get the details. Graham was probably in another state. Would I call? Text? Email? What was I going to say? I'd been asking that since I started the search, but I didn't have an answer yet.

"We're done for the day," Oz said again. "Go look, and I'll clean up."

I wanted to ask *are you sure*, but I didn't want to give him a chance to change his mind. "Thank you." I stepped to the side of the room, leaned against the wall, and pulled up the info. My heart leaped into my throat. Graham was still local. I could be there by bus in half an hour, that was how close he was.

That didn't mean it was a good idea to drop in unannounced. I didn't know anything about his life now. But looking him in the eye and apologizing was much better than a text. If he wanted me gone after that, I'd be on my way. Would he be indifferent? Hate me?

"Well?" Oz's question startled me.

I showed him the address. It spoke for itself.

"You're going over there?"

I nodded. That answered my question. My racing thoughts wouldn't slow until I did something about this.

Oz jerked his head toward the parking lot. "I'll drive."

"No. It's okay. You've got stuff to do. I won't ask you to chauffeur me around the city. I got it. I'll see you tomorrow. Thank you for everything." I was already sliding toward the door.

Oz grabbed my wrist, and a shock of heat spilled inside. "You didn't ask. You're not going alone."

I could argue, but I liked him looking out for me. Besides, if I was babbling at him, I could stay out of my own head on the trip, and we'd get there a lot faster. "Okay."

I loved Oz's truck. It was one of those big old Fords that had been around longer than me. He kept it in top shape, and it suited him perfectly. He gave me a hand up into the passenger seat, before taking his own spot.

My plan to fill the space with chatter failed. I couldn't stop my brain from the if-then loop it was stuck on over what I was supposed to say to Graham.

We got to the address on my phone way too soon. The building was an old house. Stepping inside revealed four apartment doors. Not an unusual layout for Salt Lake. The only reason my feet didn't freeze in place was I didn't want to hold Oz up.

I approached Apartment C, muttered two conflicting prayers for there to be no one home and for Graham to answer, and knocked.

fighting for it

The seconds ticked away. We should go. Locks clicked on the other side. We should have gone.

The door swung open, and Graham's wide-eyed stare landed on me. He looked incredible. Dark hair, penetrating gaze, and warmth in his hesitant smile. "Luna. What are you…? Not that I'm complaining, but why are you here? How did you find me?"

"I had a good teacher," I said shyly. "Probation is up. We can talk to each other again."

"Yeah. Who's the bodyguard?" He nodded behind me.

I glanced at Oz, before focusing on Graham again. "This is Cole. He's a friend."

"Just a friend?"

My heart hesitated but my mind spit out an immediate answer. "Yes." Impulse took over, and I threw my arms around Graham's neck. "I missed you. I'm so glad I found you."

"Me too." He returned the hug, squeezing tightly. His warmth, the scent of aftershave I still remembered years later, his voice—they were all perfect.

I should pull away, this wasn't the kind of relationship we had, but I didn't want to let go. Disappointment slipped through me when he finally released me and stepped away.

Chapter Two

Graham jerked away from me and I realized Oz had a fistful of Graham's shirt and had pinned him to the doorframe.

What the hell? "*Cole*." My exclamation came out tighter than I intended.

"This bastard ruined your life," Oz growled. "He manipulated you, he got you arrested, and I wouldn't be fucking surprised if he was grooming you from the moment he met you."

"*Whoa*." Graham held his hands up, palms out. "Grooming? Never. Besides, you knocked on my door. What is this, Luna?"

Oz stepped between us. "You're talking to me, not her."

"Stop. Please." I rested a hand on Oz's arm. "This was never his fault. I sucked him in. You know that." He was one of the few people who was familiar with all the details.

Under my fingers, Oz's grip relaxed, but his muscles stayed tense. He let go of Graham and stood next to me. *Loom* might be a more appropriate word.

fighting for it

The disruption was nasty, but it didn't erase the warmth spreading through me from the hug. From seeing Graham again. And Oz's stance certainly didn't erase the fantasies dancing in my head. If Oz weren't here, a hug could've become a kiss, leading to roaming hands, stepping inside, clothes falling off—

"I was never *grooming* you." Graham held my gaze, yanking me into reality. "You were the most brilliant student I ever had. I wanted the best for you, and I still do."

A door opened and shut behind me. "Everything okay out here?" an older woman asked.

"All good, thanks, Gracie." Graham was warm and friendly.

She frowned, then headed out the front door of the building.

"Let's go inside and talk," Graham said quietly.

"Oka—"

"Nope." Oz cut me off.

I appreciated the concern, but it didn't seem to have been the best idea to do this with him. He had a point though that I should have this conversation in a public place. I trusted Graham, but I also hadn't seen him in a few years, and I was an optimist, not an idiot. "Coffee? I saw a place a few blocks away."

Graham cast a pointed look at Oz.

A billion scenarios had run through my head about this reunion, and this was nowhere in the bunch. "Can I talk to you outside?" I asked Oz.

He joined me on the front porch, his arms crossed and an even deeper scowl than normal in place. "I don't care who approached who for help when you knew him. I don't trust him."

"You don't have to," I said. "But thank you for being here for me." It really was sweet. "And thank you for taking the time to bring me out here. I've got it from here."

"I'm not sure that's a good idea."

"I'm sure that's my decision." I smiled sweetly at him.

Oz sigh-growled. "I'll see you tomorrow. "

I waited until he was in his truck and had started the engine before heading inside. Graham was still in his doorway. "You've made some interesting friends."

"He's a good guy, I promise."

"Seems like it." Graham sounded sincere. "I understand wanting to look out for you. Coffee?"

We walked side-by-side toward the cafe. He was so close I felt the heat radiating from his arm. How did I restart this conversation? *How have you been* felt a bit weak, but what else was I supposed to say? Especially when I couldn't stop thinking about

fighting for it

that hug becoming a kiss, then roaming hands, us slipping into his apartment to lose our clothes...

In the unlikely event that Oz wanted to stay and watch, that was even better.

"This isn't at all how I thought seeing you would go." Graham's tone was impossible to read.

He'd been thinking about me? About seeing me? "How did you think it would go?"

"I thought it wouldn't. I tried to keep you from finding me."

"Oh." My step faltered and my mood did the same.

"Don't take that the way it sounds. I hoped you'd moved on. Forgotten about me."

The man who taught me half of what I know? Who actually cared that the nerdy quiet girl wanted his input on a project? Would didn't dismiss me because of my awkwardness? Who starred in *so many* of my fantasies? "Like I could."

"When I saw you on my doorstep, I— What have you been up to?" He glanced at me with a sad smile.

I... wanted to sandwich you between me and the doorframe and kiss you until you couldn't breathe. I wouldn't ask him to finish the thought because it couldn't live up to my hopes. "Odd jobs here and there. Oz— Cole has taught me a lot about the hardware side of networking. Even if probation didn't keep me from doing real programming, no one wants to hire the girl who hacked the world. But I'm getting by. Life is pretty good. You?"

As we walked, his arm brushed mine and his fingertips skittered across the back of my hand. It was a little thing, but the light contact set my never endings on fire.

"I do a lot of private tutoring... A little... It pays the bills." Graham sighed.

The last time we spoke was at the courthouse before we entered our plea bargains. Graham was convinced his career was over.

He'd recover. I had no doubt. But from inside the struggle, I understood how it could look bleak.

"Your friend is Cole Denton." Graham said the name with recognition. "You've got friends in a lot of interesting places looking out for you."

"It's nice." And it wasn't just Oz. My best friend, Violet. One of her boyfriends, Ramsey, was responsible for my reduced sentence years ago. Since Graham brought up Oz, it would be easy to gush, and I totally took that chance most of the time when it came to Oz.

Right now, I was here with Graham. A mind and man I'd looked up to for almost a decade. He wasn't my professor anymore. Hooking up with him wouldn't violate any ethics or honor codes.

fighting for it

Optimism said he was as interested as me. Experience argued otherwise.

We reached the coffee shop, Graham held the door for me, and joined me in line. Did we look like a couple to the handful of other people here? Silver was peeking through around Graham's temples—how did he feel about being thirty-nine and going gray?—and I looked young for my twenty-nine. But if I kissed him, would anyone even bat an eye?

Would he return the gesture, or freeze up? Or worst of all, push me away?

I may have a slew of fantasies about people watching while we screwed, but I didn't know if making a move was a good idea, and I definitely didn't want an audience if it wasn't.

When we had a table, tucked away in the far corner of the cafe, I'd start simple. Ask if he was interested.

Or I'd chicken out completely.

We reached the cashier. "Quad shot mocha latte?" Graham asked me. "It's on me." He remembered what I used to drink.

Did my heart just start skipping rope? Darn straight. "Peppermint tea with sugar. I'm not young and dumb enough anymore to think I can drink espresso at night and still get any sleep."

"You're not even thirty, and you were never dumb." He turned to the cashier, repeated my order, and got himself a large coffee.

I'd been joking. He was so serious sometimes. Even that was sexy.

Graham took our drinks and handed me mine. Did I fixate on that moment when his hand brushed mine? Uh, *yeah*. My imagination was working overtime tonight, and I either needed to shut it up, or get it what it wanted.

We found a table away from everyone. He held out my chair and pushed it in as I sat, then took the seat across from me. A table between us. Was that intentional? Him being polite?

"How have you been otherwise?" I asked.

He studied me with eyes so dark I could swim in them, his sturdy jaw set in that way that said he was thinking. "Good. Surviving. You?"

"Same." I didn't want to do this meaningless banter. I wanted actual answers about his actual life. "Have you been doing any modding lately?" When we started talking, way back when, that was one of the first things we realized we had in common. Graham and I both got into programming by making mods for games.

Of course, it was a totally different beast back then. I was doing it so I could play Violet's PS1 games on my computer, since my parents didn't believe in game consoles. He'd gotten into rewriting games so he could change character appearances and scenarios.

Graham shook his head, an almost-smile tugging up the corners of his mouth. "That would be a violation of my probation."

"Uh-huh." Given how much tech had changed in the last three years, and the hoops I'd had to jump through to find him, I didn't believe for a moment he'd let himself get rusty. Besides, he loved the challenge as much as I did. "Tell me another story," I teased.

"Says the woman who tracked me down."

"I didn't start looking until our probations were over." Because I wouldn't have been able to stay away if I'd found him sooner. "And you did a fantastic job of hiding yourself for someone who's been obeying the rules."

"You found me, so I didn't do that great a job."

"Your words, not mine." My tone was playful. This was what I missed. Looking at Graham was nice, but the ease of our conversations… I'd craved that.

He let his grin break through. "I *have* been working on a theory, and I'd like your input."

"Of course." My excitement rose another notch. Whether he was talking about technology or something else, I was in for wherever the tangents took us.

"If a balrog ran a restaurant, where would he put it?"

Chibi Luna clapped with glee in my head. "Trick question?" This was a game we used to play all the time, spawned from the fact that the only things most Final Fantasy games had in common were the name, the crystals, and the elementals. That conversation had become a challenge to fit all sorts of unrelated worlds together.

"Completely serious. Why?" Graham asked.

Because the answer was obvious. "Hell's Kitchen."

He groaned, but his smile never wavered. "And Luke Cage is his head chef, because he's the only person in the world the balrog doesn't accidentally set on fire?"

"They have a super low crime rate." I ran with the idea. "He's basically an unofficial Continental"—like in John Wick—"where no business is allowed on his grounds. Someone called him on the rule once, and he enforced it. No one's questioned his authority since."

Graham leaned in. "But he's got a soft spot for the neighborhood kids." Amusement and excitement bubbled in his voice. "They love his place at Halloween. Best. Candy. Ever."

Because a balrog chef would make the best treats. "Popcorn balls with a lot of cinnamon and a hint of habanero. Plus, he'd rock the decorations, walking that fine line between terrifying and whimsical." I could picture it, and the imagery made me laugh with delight. "The kids scream in terror when Mr. Balrog jump scares them, and they all love every minute of it." Everything about this made me giggle.

My laugh died when I realized how intensely Graham watched me.

"You look good." His serious tone was back.

Geez I wanted him to kiss me. Did he really think I looked good? That wasn't the kind of thing people said to just be polite. This was a key reason I didn't like small talk. I wanted to assume everyone was sincere.

"You look good too." The words tumbled past my lips. I couldn't take them back now. Screw this. I rose on my toes, leaned over the table, and pressed my lips to his.

When he didn't return the kiss, my blood ran cold and my face scorched flaming hot.

Before I could pull away, Graham slid his hand to my neck and held me captive as he deepened the kiss. He worked his mouth hungrily over mine, devouring my soft whimpers and licking away my doubt.

This blew fantasy out of the water, and it was only a kiss. The kind of toe-curling attention that made my blood sing and would keep me warm for a long time, all by itself. I gripped the edge of the table for balance. Were people watching?

If so, I hoped they enjoyed this almost as much as I was.

When Graham broke away, I gasped, and forced my jaw not to keep working. I licked my lips inside, like he'd done seconds before.

He let me go and sank into his seat. His frown was the frigid polar opposite of what I felt. "I'm sorry, Luna, I can't."

I stared at him in disbelief, waiting for him to finish the sentence. *I can't... wait to get you back to my place and get naked. I can't... believe we had to be apart this long.* Nope. He was done talking.

"You can't... be serious."

He raked his fingers through thick, dark hair. "I'm the last thing you need in your life."

Chapter Three

My disbelief clawed toward something darker. "I can decide for myself who I do and don't want in my life."

"What about Tiff?" He held my gaze, unflinching, and my irritation inched closer to anger at my college girlfriend's name. "You're so sweet. Always seeing the best in people. I'm a disgraced college professor who may never teach again. It doesn't matter that my probation is over—the world sees what happens the same way your *friend* does. You need someone better—"

"*Stop.*" I couldn't keep the edge from my voice. I was willing to overlook a lot of things. Give people the benefit of the doubt. But no one else got to tell me what was best for me. My parents did that to me in high school. Refused to let me skip grades or take early college courses. Told me to suck it up when I complained about being bored and then about being bullied. Pointed out again and again that if I was going to survive in *the real world,* it was best for me to learn to be like everyone else.

"This was a mistake." I shoved away from the table. My face had to be bright red from anger and humiliation. I needed to be anywhere but here. "You're right. I shouldn't have found you. Have a great life."

"Luna, sit down." Graham grabbed my wrist and I jerked away harder than I needed to, slamming my hand into a nearby chair and sending it skidding a few inches. The sting added to the growing lump in my throat. I stalked toward the door, not daring to look back. I had to keep my gaze focused on the next steps. Reaching the sidewalk. Heading for the bus stop, which, thankfully, was nearby, and the bus was only a couple blocks away.

"Luna." Graham reached for me again.

I glared at him, pouring all my fury into the look. "Touch me, and I'll scream," I said evenly. I might scream anyway. Not really. Composure was important in public. But *wow* I wanted to lose control.

Graham stayed about a foot away. "I didn't mean—"

I slipped in my earbuds and turned away. As humiliated and pissed off as I was, I was still worried that if I let him explain, I'd believe him and forgive him. He was right—sometimes I was a shitty judge of character, and I didn't want any more hints that was true when it came to him.

fighting for it

The bus pulled up to the curb, saving me from having to pretend any longer that I could ignore Graham. I stepped on, and he let me go.

That shouldn't hurt. It was exactly what I wanted.

I took a seat at the rear of the bus, tucked away from prying eyes, and pretended to be involved in my phone. The screen wasn't on, and neither was the music. I couldn't stop replaying the entire coffee shop scene with Graham.

Did I overreact? I was as embarrassed as I was mad, but that didn't give him the right to tell me this was for my own good. Why didn't he just say *I'm not interested*? That would've hurt. A lot. But putting the whole thing on me.

And kissing me, first…

When I got home, I slunk into my basement studio apartment. The space was cramped, barely big enough for a full-sized bed and a desk, but it was cheap and I didn't take up much space. Violet had offered to let me stay in her apartment when she moved in with Hunter. She'd let the lease auto-renew. I already owed her and her guys too much I could never repay.

I flopped down on my bed and stared at the ceiling. Speaking of Violet, I promised I'd call her when I found Graham. She'd make me feel better in an instant if I did.

I wasn't ready to feel better yet. I needed to process before I shared this with anyone, and especially before Violet insisted on hammering on Graham's door on my behalf, to tell him he was an idiot.

The next few hours passed in a zombie-like haze. I streamed *Fruits Basket* to remind me I wasn't the only clueless girl in the world who was attracted to an even more clueless guy, when there were plenty of other attractive men around me.

When I finally lay down for the night to sleep, I wanted to indulge in one of my favorite fantasies, with my favorite battery-operated boyfriend. An orgasm would make things better.

It was a scene I'd played out a billion times since Graham was my professor, and it never got old. I'd separated fantasy from reality then, and I could now. It would be easy to slide into the familiar scene.

A computer lab with just the two of us. We'd be working closer than we should be, and he'd push me onto a nearby empty space on a desk. Slide between my legs. Cup my face in his palms, and say, *"I'm the last thing you need in your life."*

Damn it. My frustration returned, bubbling inside.

I could deal with this. It was my imagination after all. I'd make a few alterations and it would become another of my favorite daydreams. The one

fighting for it

where Oz walked in on us mid-screw, liked what he saw, and fucked my face while Graham pounded me from behind.

A good, hard, dirty round of everyone getting off, complete with the thrill of being in a public place.

In my mind, I rewound to before Graham opened his stupid mouth. While he was seconds from kissing me. The imaginary classroom door opened.

"I hope I'm interrupting," Oz said in that delicious tenor.

"I'm glad you have people looking out for you. I'm the last thing you need in your life," Graham repeated.

I yanked my pillow out from under my head, smothered my face with it, and screamed until I was hoarse and out of breath.

Stupid jerk had to go and think he was being noble and ruin everything.

———

I felt better the next morning. Amazing what a good night's sleep could do for clarity. Besides, I'd see Oz this morning, he'd sign off on me completing my apprenticeship, and then I'd stop by Loading Java and visit Violet and have ice cream and coffee for lunch. I was an adult; I could make decisions like that. I wasn't going to mix them together or anything. Though, if it was the right kind of ice cream…

I picked out a black pencil skirt, and a button-down teal blouse to go with it. There was no on-site work today, and this made me feel pretty and professional. I also paid more attention to my makeup than usual—blush, eyeliner, and lipstick, instead of just a dash of mascara and lip gloss.

An actual job may be out of my grasp right now, but I could dress for success. Tell myself if Graham could see me, he'd be sorry he was an ass.

Not that he deserved any more space in my head. Nope, I was banishing him from my thoughts. He was a silly little girl's silly little crush, and I was far too proudly weird to simply be called *silly*.

The outfit did more for my confidence than I expected, especially with the appreciative glances I drew as I got on the bus. The trip was spent sifting through job postings. I wasn't a convicted felon anymore, and I had wicked programming skills. I could own any of these positions.

I reached the building where Oz's apprenticeship company had its headquarters and headed for the entrance. The steel and glass structure was four stories of simplicity in the middle of an office park that was a lot the same. Oz's office sat on the first floor, near the rear entrance. The most understated suite here.

fighting for it

Few people had any idea he owned the entire business park.

The assistant working reception smiled at me when I walked in. "Cole is waiting for you. Go on back," Holly waved me down the hallway.

I walked the familiar, industrial grade carpet. This was the last time I'd do so as an *apprentice* and there was a sense of accomplishment in the thought. Oz's door was open, and I knocked lightly on the frame.

He glanced up from his computer, raised an eyebrow, and gestured to the table in the opposite corner of his desk. "Come on in."

I liked this room. Not just because it was his, but it had warmth. Personality. Richly stained furniture. Photos of his family on matching wood bookshelves—his parents, his sister, her kids. Him with all of them. There were also pictures of him with some of his former Rinslet colleagues. The only indicator here that he had anything to do with the other company.

Oz stepped past me to close the door, then took the chair next to mine at a table big enough to sit four or five. He slid a manila folder to me. "This is your certificate of completion. All your finalized paperwork. It's been wonderful working with you, and I'm always available for a reference."

"Same. I mean, thank you. I mean…" *Sigh.* "You know what I mean." Such a dork.

Oz smiled. A rare sight, and as alluring as most everything else he did. "I do. Any questions for me about this?"

I shook my head. That was a safe way to answer.

"Then your apprenticeship is officially over." He stood and offered his hand.

I rose as well and shook it. His grip was firm and warm. When he let go, and moved a finger to my chin, my heart leaped into my throat.

He lifted my head and searched my face. "This feels like an asshole move, doing this right after what happened last night." His voice rumbled over me.

"I don—"

Oz brushed his lips over mine, and my mind stalled. What in the what? He drew his thumb along my cheek as he cupped my face, tilting his head to lean into the kiss. He was tender but unapologetic, the way he introduced his tongue to mine.

When he pulled away, I couldn't find my voice.

"Luna?"

"Wow." In my head, a chibi me was clapping and dancing and squealing.

His smile was back. "You're not going to slap me for waiting until there was another guy in the picture?"

fighting for it

Double what? He couldn't mean Graham. That assumption needed to be corrected post-haste. "There's no other guy."

"Sure." Oz still cradled my face—that felt so good. "There are days when you talk non-stop about Graham, and he never stopped looking at you last night."

Because Graham was the asshole. I frowned.

"What's wrong?" Oz asked.

I didn't want to get into this now, but I didn't want to hide anything, either. If Oz didn't like what he heard, it was better he have a chance to back out now. "There's nothing. I guarantee it. I kissed him last night."

A frown whispered across Oz's face and vanished behind his more typical mask of blankness.

"You're right." I needed to keep this brief. To not ramble. "I do—did—like him, and he pushed me away, *for my own good.*" The idea still pissed me off.

Damn Oz's unreadable expression. He could've given me a *never mind*, or *good for him*, or *I'll kill the idiot bastard.* Instead, silence stretched between us.

Should I pull away? I screwed up twice in a row, didn't I?

"What did you do?" Oz asked.

"Told him he was a jerk and left."

"Do you have a problem with what I just did?"

That freaking amazing kiss? "Are you going to tell me you waited until now, for my own good?"

"I'm going to tell you that your probation is over, and so's your apprenticeship. I'm not your *boss* anymore, so it's no longer inappropriate for me to let you know how desperately I want you," Oz said.

Brain freeze. If Graham had done everything wrong last night, Oz was saying everything right this morning. I could kiss him, but I wasn't over the humiliation of the last time I tried that.

"I'm not an idiot." Oz traced a short path over my neck with his fingertips. "I don't expect that if you have feelings for him, they're gone. You don't need to swear forever to me, or even exclusivity. Yet. Keep a place for me on your calendar."

My tongue was stuck to the roof of my mouth. I licked my lips, trying to get them to form words, but it didn't work.

"Tell me what you're thinking." Oz's tone was one of command.

"I really want you to kiss me again."

He slanted his mouth over mine, and consumed me in a toe-curling, tonsil-tickling kiss.

Chapter Four

Oz turned and nudged me, then lifted me to sit on the table, barely breaking our lip lock.

My skirt was too tight for him to push between my legs, but he fiddled with the hem as he rested his thigh against mine.

"Pinch me?" I whimpered against his lips.

He slid his palm over my bare skin, to between my legs, and pinched the tender flesh of my inner thighs.

I moaned at the sharp sting and the desire it sent spilling through me. "Nope. Not dreaming."

He chuckled dryly. "It's real. Is that the only reason you asked?"

"Yes. But it won't be the only reason next time." The pain had numbed quickly, but the tingle lingered.

Oz pulled away to tug at the edges of my blouse, near the buttons. "You always look incredible, but today you had to go and wear something that makes you easy to unwrap." He fiddled with the first button, teasing my skin underneath.

"I wouldn't say no." Did I sound desperate or sexy? Did I care?

Oz shook his head and kissed along my jaw, down to my collarbone, stopping at the first button on my top, before pulling away, until the only contact he made was lightly grasping my fingertips. "If I didn't have another meeting in thirty. I wanted to plan this better, leave us more time, but I was running out of it."

"Because of Graham?" I didn't like my ambivalence at his name.

"Partly. But also because I want to take you out. A date—so there's no question—and this is short notice, but it would be tonight. I had planned to skip the event, but a friend asked me to attend--"

"You need a date for something you don't want to go to?" That wasn't so sexy, but I was missing something.

There was his smile again. I could get used to that, especially if he only used it around me. "It's an industry thing. While I'd rather keep you to myself for the next several days, at least, this is a chance for you to meet people. You're brilliant and this can open doors for you."

The circuits met in my brain, completing the connection, and realization flowed in. "The Konsoles for Kids auction?" I couldn't think of anything else to say. The event was huge in tech. Some of the biggest names auctioned off rare collectibles to raise money for Primary Children's Hospital. Oz wanted to introduce me to those people? "I'm not great with the whole meeting people thing."

"You're great with me." He squeezed my fingers.

It was totally different. "I know you. You get me."

"And I'll be there with you. Admittedly, showing off the genius cutie who let me kiss her on my conference table, but this is about you, not me. It's a costume party, but a lot of people will be wearing normal clothes. It's a casual event."

Why was I hesitating? Because I didn't want a repeat of last night. Not that I was going to kiss anyone there except Oz, but I was plenty capable of embarrassing myself in other ways. This was a chance of a lifetime, though.

"Yes or no?" Oz asked.

"Yes." Saying it felt good. My shock was wearing off, leaving a hopped-up girl who'd had three quad shot mochas dancing in my brain and screaming with joy. "Yes, yes, yes."

Oz scooted me off the table and bent in for one more long kiss. He brushed his thumb over my bottom lip before stepping away. "I'll pick you up at seven. I'd ask you to stay, but…"

"Meeting. I know. See you tonight." My voice tilted up at the end, and I hid my wince.

It took the last of my restraint to keep from skipping out of his office, down the hall, and outside. The instant I hit the sidewalk, several yards from the building, I let out a tiny squeal and clapped.

I had to call Violet. I needed to share this with someone. As I grabbed her number and listened to the phone ring, I walked past the bus stop. There would be another one.

"Hey." Violet's voice was bright.

"So glad you didn't send me to voicemail. We need to talk. Can you talk now? I can call back."

"Hang on, I'll go on break." Violet's voice grew muffled as she spoke to someone in the background. During the days she managed an anime themed gaming cafe, and in her free time—don't ask me how she managed that with two boyfriends—she volunteered at an LGBTQ+ youth homeless shelter.

I heard the faint sound of footsteps, and then a door closing. "Okay. What's up?" Violet asked.

I swallowed another squeal. Where to start? "So, last night I found Graham, and it was a *disaster*. I threw myself at him. He pushed me away."

"I'm sorry, L."

"No, it's okay. I'm over that." Or I'd put it behind me far enough it wasn't going to fuck with my mood now. "You know how my apprenticeship ended, and I knew something else would come along, but it hasn't yet? So, I was talking to Cole this morning," *talking. Ha.* "And he kissed me. Like full-on, tongue down my throat, made my toes curl… wowza. So good. And not only that, but he wants me to meet his friends." I couldn't talk fast enough. "Colleagues? It's not like a meet-the-family thing. But he wants to introduce me to people at the Konsoles for Kids auction. I don't know what to do. What am I supposed to wear? Oh, my God, Violet. Oz asked me out. Cole-freaking-Denton."

"I've got you covered," Violet said. "And I told you so." She did. She'd tried to convince me more than once that the attraction went both ways. "As soon as work's over, I'll be there. Does that give you time?"

Aside from the fact that I'd be freaking out alone for the next couple of hours? "Yes. You're the best. Seriously."

"You'd do the same for me. Until I get there?"

"Yeah?"

"No coffee. No sugar."

I stuck my tongue out at the phone, but she knew me too well. "Yes, ma'am."

Even with the bus stopping every five minutes, by the time I got home, it wasn't even eleven in the morning. Violet would be here around three thirty.

How was I supposed to keep myself occupied until then?

Washing my hair twice in one day was a bad idea, but I could shave *everything* from my armpits down. Wishful thinking? More like the power of positivity.

That didn't take nearly as much time as I'd hoped it would. I pulled on some basic underwear and a T-shirt, and spent the next few hours distracting myself with job hunting—sending off more resumes and sifting through listings. By tomorrow I may have a couple of names to drop or new people to reach out to, but no reason to ignore the existing opportunities.

Violet showed up right on time, which was still way too long for me. I let her in, and she handed me a garment bag.

"Lyn borrowed something from Sadie. You're going to love it," Violet said. Lyn was her boss at Loading Java, and Sadie—who was a brilliant professional cosplay seamstress—was one of her best friends.

I already loved it and I hadn't seen it yet. I hung the bag on the bar in the portable closet next to my bed and dragged the zipper down. Inside was a Japanese schoolgirl outfit—pleated skirt, short sleeved top, and kerchief. It was straight out of an anime. I loved it more now.

fighting for it

Even better, I didn't have to put on uncomfortable lace panties and bra. White cotton was appropriate, and I was already wearing my cutest set.

"Distract me," I said as I stripped out of my other clothes. Violet and I had changed in front of each other dozens of times. This was nothing.

"How?"

"I don't care." I unclipped the skirt from its hanger and pulled it up my legs. "Cute stories about Hunter. Ramsey's plans for world domination. Anything." The skirt rested perfectly at the top of my hips when I zipped it up. I moved on to the top.

Violet was waiting with the neckerchief. "We're adding new VR tech to the cafe. Lyn's converting a room, and we're getting the hardware straight from the manufacturer, the day it releases."

"Which means you're going to have it before release." Tech was the best distraction. It almost helped me sit still while we tied the accessories in place.

Violet headed into the bathroom, calling "maybe" over her shoulder. She returned a heartbeat later with a comb, hair elastics, and a scrunchie.

The hardware wouldn't be out for nine months, but the specs on it were unreal. I couldn't wait to get my hands on it. "I'll be your best friend if you let me play with it early."

"You're already my best friend." Damn her and her logic. She tugged the comb through my hair, and I felt her sectioning off pieces for a braid.

I already knew she was going to say yes, though. "Please, please, please, please, *pleeeeeeeaaaaassseeeee*. If you say yes, I won't subject you to the detailed specs again."

Violet laughed. "You can tell me as many times as you want. I won't understand any more than I have so far. What you should do instead, is whisper those sexy nothings in Cole's ear."

"Not sure ARM processing is bedroom talk."

"With the two of you? Are you sure?"

"Fair point." It was pretty sexy that Cole would listen to me go off about things like that, and get it.

Violet set the comb on my desk and pointed me toward the mirror on my bathroom door.

As I took in my reflection, a girl with pale skin, a single braid of red, wide eyes, and way too much implied innocence stared back. "I look like jailbait." I was already going out with a man a decade older than me. Would this make him question that? I didn't care for the surge of doubt.

Violet met my gaze in the reflection. "You look fuckable, and of consenting age. Cole knows who he asked out."

"I'm supposed to be making business connections." I tugged at the hem of my skirt. I wanted her to convince me this was okay, because she was right, I also looked good.

Violet lightly slapped my hands down. "If they don't love you for your brain, they don't deserve you."

Even I wasn't the kind of optimist who could let that go unchallenged. "You know it doesn't work that way." A book wasn't always judged by its cover, but the odds certainly leaned in that direction.

"I know that it should. I won't be hurt if you want to wear something else, but I wouldn't have brought this if I thought it wasn't right." Violet's gaze, as she stared at me in the mirror, and her tone carried her sincerity.

I smoothed out the blouse and skirt. "I really do look good."

"*Duh.*"

I'd wear the outfit. There was plenty else for me to freak out about tonight anyway, like a first date with a man I practically worshiped, to meet his work colleagues and hopefully leave the right kind of impression on all of them that I didn't make myself even more of a pariah in the industry.

Chapter Five

Violet left fifteen minutes before Oz was supposed to show up. She gave me a hug and reminded me I was going to have an amazing night.

Fortunately, Oz was early, so I only had to panic with my own thoughts for about ten minutes.

On the drive there, I babbled. I didn't even know what about, but he listened and responded, like always. I was almost calm when we arrived.

The auction was being held in an event hall at the local convention center. A few people milled outside the doors, but most were in the room itself, which was decorated with neon and steel and looked so cheesy '80's. It was *brilliant*.

"Cole." A woman called from behind us.

Oz wrapped an arm around my waist as we spun. The gesture felt possessive, and I liked it. Especially when he pointed us toward a gorgeous brunette. She was probably Oz's age, and absolutely rocking a Wonder Woman costume. I'd never have the boobs and hips to pull off a look like that, but she owned it.

fighting for it

Her smile as we approached was warm, but something about it felt insincere. *No.* That wasn't the right word, but there was something under her expression that I couldn't pinpoint. "Didn't know if you'd make it," she said.

"Why would I miss an industry event, Judy?" Oz asked.

A scowl crossed her face but vanished in a blink. Was I projecting because someone pretty wanted my date's attention?

"This is Luna." Oz nodded, never letting go of me. "Next big name in gaming."

Heat flooded my face.

"I don't doubt it." She extended her hand. "I'm Judith—not Judy—Senior VP of New Product Development at Rinslet, Inc. Pleasure to meet you." Her handshake was firm.

"The pleasure is mine." Whatever vibe I got earlier must have been a fluke, because she was nothing but sincerity now. I liked her, and with a title like that, she had to have knowledge. "I'd love to pick your brain someday."

"Same." Judith jerked a thumb at the two men standing nearby. "Brandon, my Director of Sound Engineering, and Dustin, one of my top artists."

Brandon shook my hand then Oz's. "I didn't think the Wizard ever came out from behind his curtain."

"I make exceptions under the right circumstances." Oz's voice was tight, even for him. Where did the shift in mood come from?

Dustin's gaze was fixed on me. "You must be the right circumstances." The way he studied me, it was like he was hoping to figure out what was inside. He grasped my fingers and kissed the tips.

How was I supposed to react to that?

Oz tightened his grip and pulled me closer, and I was grateful. He looked between the two men. "Rumor is you have your fingers in new things, Judy."

Judith laughed lightly. "I do, but it's not either of these two. Rather, they work for me, but there's no fingering. How much have you heard?"

"No details, but if you're involved, I know you always want the best talent." Oz didn't look fazed by the innuendo.

"It's not that kind of opportunity," Judith said. "If it were, I'd move Luna to the top of my list."

Three more people joined us. The two men were dressed in sleeveless vests, similar to Brandon's, and the woman was in a platinum blond wig, a crop-top, and low-rise jeans.

"No Doubt?" I asked.

The new woman grinned and elbowed the guy closest. "Told you someone would get it." The four of them had matching spade tattoos, like an ace of

fighting for it

spades, on their biceps. Pretty sure that wasn't part of the outfits.

Before we could do another round of introductions, someone else pulled Oz away.

So many people wanted his time, and he introduced me to every one of them. The names blurred together in my mind, but nobody questioned when I wanted their pictures to go with their business cards. I hoped I'd be able to sort it all out later.

Everything up for auction was in acrylic cases around the room, with reserves listed, and QR codes to scan and place silent bids.

"If it's not the wizard himself," a man behind us said.

I knew that voice. How? Oz and I turned, and I had to force my jaw to not drop open.

"Didn't expect to see you here." Scott McAllister was one of the two owners and founders of Rinslet, Inc, and an absolute personal hero. He was tall—then again, most people were to me—and built like a football player. His hair was graying around the temples, and he had that whole sexy silver fox vibe going on. "Who convinced you to step out from behind the curtain?"

Oz shook his hand. "Dorothy."

"She's good at that." Scott nodded. I didn't understand the reference. We hadn't met a Dorothy tonight. He'd never mentioned one before. Who—

"This is Luna." Oz pointed Scott toward me.

He turned a warm smile in my direction, and I barely had the brainpower to hold out my hand. If I were an anime character, my eyes would be huge right now, and I'd be swooning and thinking *he's so cool*.

"Hi." My voice squeaked out, and I hid a wince. "Nice to meet you." *Understatement of the freaking century*. Chibi-me was dying of a stardom overdose.

"I've heard a lot about you." Scott's grip was warm and firm when he shook my hand.

The whispers around us seemed to intensify. My imagination was really working overtime. Oz had talked about me? To Scott. Fucking. McAllister? Geez, it wasn't about my crimes was it? This was where I should say *all of it good, I hope*, but my vocal cords had frozen.

My phone vibrated through my purse and against my hip. I ignored it. Violet knew where I was, and she'd wait.

"You're really the mind behind building a patch for one of the worst pieces of malware ever." Scott shook my hand a second time. "It's a pleasure."

If I died right now, on Oz's arm, Scott shaking my hand, I'd be happy. Dark thought. But not really. I was such a freaking fangirl. I found my voice. "The pleasure is definitely mine."

"Of course it is." Scott grinned.

fighting for it

Luna.

Did someone just whisper my name? More than once? Did endorphins cause hallucinations?

A woman a little older than me joined us, and Scott wrapped an arm around her waist. Her blond hair fell in soft curls around her face. She was the kind of elegant I'd never be, and she carried herself like she knew it.

Perfect complement to Scott.

"Cole. I heard you were here. Had to see it myself," she said.

"Hey, Kenzie. It's been too long." Oz's tone was more formal with her. Not in a bad way—more in a *we're not close* kind of way.

Scott squeezed her hip. They were adorable together. "Kenz, this is Luna."

"*Oh.*" Kenzie's composure slipped, and my gut plummeted. "Lovely to meet you." She was all smiles again."

"What was with the slip?" Scott's question mirrored the one in my thoughts.

"It really is lovely to meet you, I was just surprised to hear your name." Kenzie frowned as she looked at me. "I say this because you're a friend of Cole's"—

That sounded *so* not good.

—"I'm the queen of composure, and I don't know if I could keep mine right now. All my respect," Kenzie said.

"Wait. What?" Was I just insulted? The words weren't delivered in a cruel way. Was she talking about the outfit? It was a mistake, wasn't it?

Kenzie reached for her purse. "You don't know. The anniversary article…"

My world was falling away, leaving me dangling in mid-air with no support. The whispers around us were louder than I'd realized. People were looking at us.

Kenzie handed me her phone. The headline on the screen said *10th Anniversary of the Hack that Brought the World to Its Knees*. A photo of me, complete with my name, was front and center.

The room spun around me. Now that I was paying attention to the whispers, it was clear what they were about.

Is that really her?

Fucking idiot.

They let someone like her in the door?

"I need some air." I broke away before I could hear anyone's answer, and cut a straight line for the nearest door, walking as fast as possible without breaking into a run.

Chapter Six

Since we were a block from the dead center of the city, there weren't many places for me to escape to. I settled myself on a stone bench near a clump of trees, set away from the street, and breathed in the exhaust-filled air.

That didn't comfort me in any sense of the word.

Oz sat next to me, his thigh pressing into mine. "Hey." He covered my hand.

"Did you hear them in there?" I tried to keep the panic from my voice. People were supposed to forget about what I'd done. This was my chance at a fresh start. A new career. *Finally.* "They were calling me an idiot. A criminal. Worse." Things I didn't want to think about, let alone repeat.

"They don't know you. I do, and you're none of those things. Others will feel the same."

"I don't want to spend my time explaining myself, over and over. Especially if they've already decided I'm the villain."

"That's fair."

Panic was already fading, but it didn't leave me with any answers as it passed. "I know it'll be okay, it's just… It's a shock. I was putting this behind me."

"Do you want to leave?"

I didn't want my time with him to be over.

"Would you rather go inside again?" Oz asked.

"No. Please no."

"We can camp out here for tonight. I'll have someone bring a tent and sleeping bag." He sounded completely serious.

For all I knew, he was, and it made me smile. "I'm having a lot of fun with you. If we go, you'll take me home, I'll sit up all night, overthinking things and not coming up with solutions, and I don't want to go home to an empty apartment and be alone with my thoughts."

Oz tilted my chin up to look me in the eye. "So I'll go home with you, and you won't be alone." He brushed his lips over mine. "Because I'm having a lot of fun, too."

Back at my place, I realized just how tiny my apartment was when Oz joined me inside. I should've thought this through better.

"What's with the frown?" He asked.

"It's a little cramped in here."

He stepped closer. "I'll have to snuggle you close, then." A husky growl ran through his already deep voice. He teased the hem of my skirt, pushing it higher and tickling my thighs. "If I didn't already, this outfit would make me feel like a dirty old man."

"What if I like dirty older men?" I certainly did when they looked and thought like him.

"Lucky for me. Speaking of, did you ever fantasize about Graham? Have naughty dreams?"

All the freaking time. No way was I telling the man standing in my apartment, reaching his hand under my dress, that I diddled myself to thoughts of someone else.

"It's not a trap." Oz drew his mouth up the side of my neck, his hot breath sending goosebumps racing over my skin. "I want to hear what kind of filthy fucking thoughts you have."

"So, so many." Was it okay to say that out loud?"

He dragged a thumb over my bottom lip. "Don't stop talking now. How about me? What kind of things are you fantasizing about me doing to you?"

My eyes were wide and my imagination was inches away from hopping the tracks to be heard. I shook my head, unable to speak.

He pushed his thumb into my mouth, and I sucked instinctively.

"I'm here because I like the things you say and the way you think," he said. "What kind of things are you thinking about me with you. Tell me." There was a distinct thread of command in his tone.

"There is one I have a lot…" If I didn't say it, it was unlikely I could have it.

"See? Tell me. What kind of daydreams make Luna wet?"

My heart hammered against my ribs and my pulse raced. What if he thought I was a freak?

Then he wasn't for me? "That you're rough."

"Rough how?" He grabbed my wrist tightly, and I gasped

Here went nothing. "That you know it's okay to pin me down and take what you want. Fuck my face. Finger me until I beg to come. Stretch me out with your cock and fuck me until my legs don't work." Was that too much? "And then cuddle with me after."

Oz's smile was almost feral. Frightening and enticing. "Do you actually want that, or are you content with it staying fantasy?"

"I actually want that."

He moved his mouth to my ear, his hot break searing my skin. "You tell me to stop, and I will," he said.

"Okay."

Gentle Oz vanished as he shoved up my skirt and pushed my panties aside. He plunged two fingers inside me. "Fucking hell, you're wet." He pumped, in and out, sliding easily against my slick skin until my hips thrust in time with his movement.

fighting for it

My body swayed with the rhythm of hard and fast. I gasped in surprise when he pulled out without warning.

He shoved his fingers in my mouth. "Tell me how you taste," he ordered.

I spent my time sucking each finger clean, relishing his groans and my taste. "So, so good."

Oz knotted his fingers in my hair and yanked back my head. He crushed his mouth to mine. I could drown in the need that reverberated through me as he probed my mouth with his tongue.

"You really do." He groaned against my skin when he pulled away. "You do magical things with that tongue." Hand still in my hair, he forced me to the ground, undoing his pants with his free hand. He freed himself, and I whimpered at how big he was. Almost too big.

"This is what you do to me every time I think about you. Every time I hear you talk," he said. "And now I find out you've got a filthy mind hiding under all that sugar. I need to feel your dirty mouth on my cock." He pressed into my mouth without warning, holding me close, driving deep enough I almost gagged.

I'd never been so turned on. I wanted him to use me. To get off on me being his dirty little girl. To take what he wanted and make sure I got the same.

As he thrust against my face, I swirled my tongue around his thick shaft, relishing his taste and his groan. His movements grew shorter. His grunts deeper and more punctuated.

I met his gaze, eyes wide, not sure if I wanted him to finish now, and cover my face, or draw things out longer.

He let out a shuddering breath as he pulled away. My chin was wet with drool. My eyes watered. I needed more.

Oz yanked me to my feet again, and tore away my panties, leaving a rough burn where the fabric tore. He shoved his fingers between my legs again, but didn't penetrate me this time.

"Fuck, you're dripping." The gravel in his voice was enticing. "You're a filthy slut, aren't you?"

If he'd said that in any other circumstance, I'd be furious. The language was part of the play, though, and in the moment, it turned me on even more. I nodded my head. "Yes."

"If your teacher friend was here, and I made him watch, would that make you even wetter? I bet you practically come at the thought."

Geez, Graham watching us. Getting off on this as much as we were? "Yes."

Oz threw me on the bed and forced his thigh between my legs, prying them open. He pressed his knee into my pussy, and shoved my shirt and bra out

fighting for it

of the way. He kneaded my breasts and pinched my nipples. Tugging hard. Twisting until the sting ached all over. Until my hips were bucking and I was grinding against his leg, desperate for more.

He dipped his head near mine. "Beg me for it."

"Let me come, please?" I was so fucking turned on.

He moved his hand from my breasts to press against my throat. "Make me believe you want it."

My head fuzzed and I floated into the clouds. "Please?"

"What would you have done if I felt you up in front of everyone at the party tonight?"

Oh, fuck. Just when I thought my pulse couldn't race any faster. "Let you."

"Because you like the idea of all those eyes on you."

I nodded.

"Say it."

My throat was so dry. I licked my lips. "At night, I finger myself to the fantasy of a roomful of people watching you fuck me."

"Because?"

"Because I'm a dirty, cock hungry slut." Things I'd only ever muttered in my own head. Things I didn't expect to ever say to someone else.

And the way Oz watched me, I'd say it again and again.

He tightened his grip on my throat and moved his other hand between my legs, to glide his fingers inside me again.

The penetration was incredible, but it wasn't going to get me off. My clit begged for attention and my thoughts were made of cotton candy.

"Finger me, please?" I *begged*. "Play with my clit until I come."

He slid his fingers out of me and up, to tease my swollen bud as he lightly choked me. I was teetering so precariously on the edge that it didn't take much to push me over into orgasm.

Climax racked my body, shuddering through me until my body was too sensitive to take anymore. I tried to pull away, but he didn't let up. I squirmed. This was too much, but it was also incredible.

Oz finally eased up.

I barely had enough time to draw a breath, before he rolled a condom on and thrust his cock inside me. He pinned my knees to my chest, gripping my thigh with one hand, and moving his thumb back to my clit.

He built to a slow rhythm, easing off each time I drew close to orgasm again, then pushing harder, both with the fucking and the fingering.

"God, your cunt's so fucking tight." He sounded like he was on the edge of losing control.

I squeezed around him, delighting in his groan.

fighting for it

He increased his pressure on my clit, stroking until I came again, clenching hard, spasming with him buried inside me. He thrust harder. Faster. Slamming against me with abandon. Pushing me deeper and deeper into pleasure.

I was lost in all of it when his stuttered grunts reached me, and he gave a few final thrusts, before slowing to a stop.

Our breathing was the only sound in the room for several seconds. Oz let go of my legs and rested his hands on either side of my head as he brushed his lips lightly over mine.

"You're so incredible," he murmured.

I might have blushed at that, but my skin must already be flushed and bright pink from the exertion.

He kissed me again. "Don't move."

I couldn't if I wanted to.

He vanished into the bathroom, and a moment later he returned with a washcloth. He was so gentle as wiped my face clean, and then moved between my legs.

There was no way we were both going to fit in my bed, but he made it work, pulling me into him and holding me tight.

I rested my forehead on his chest and danced my fingers over his skin, memorizing every texture and letting myself be wrapped in this cocoon of warmth and security.

"Is that a typical fantasy for you?" He asked softly.

"They run the gamut, but there are a lot of variations on that."

He kissed the top of my head. "So many things to learn about you. So many delicious, incredible things."

———

"You expecting company?" Oz's voice had that deep, sleepy sexy tone to it.

Amazing way to wake up. Too bad the knocking on the door got to me first. "Never. Probably Violet to take me to breakfast. Get the deets."

"Mmm." Oz pulled me tighter into him, his cock pressing into my ass and his palm teasing higher up my rib cage. "Too bad for her. I'm having you for breakfast."

"She'll understand." I didn't want to leave the bed yet, though. "What's the etiquette about texting my best friend, if she's standing a few yards away, because I don't want to get up?" Why hadn't Violet texted me? She always let me know when she was coming over.

Oz kissed me on the top of the head, and managed to extract himself from the sheets without

fighting for it

disturbing me too much. "I'll tell her. Unless you have an issue with that."

"None at all." I liked the idea quite a bit. I reached for my phone out of habit, as he pulled on his jeans.

Yup, there was a text from Violet.

Oz crossed the short distance to the door, and undid the chain and deadbolt.

I opened the message, to find a photo of Oz's truck in my driveway, with a kissy face, a peach, an eggplant, and the words, *Call me later.*

That wasn't Violet on the other side of the door Oz was currently opening.

"Morning." Oz's voice was flatter than normal.

"Morning." *Graham.* "Let me talk to Luna. I need to apologize."

Chapter Seven

Oz swung the door shut.

I should be mad that he did so without asking me first, but I didn't want to see Graham.

"Luna." Graham's voice was muffled as he knocked again.

He'd said he wanted to apologize.

Why did it matter? I had Oz now, even if I didn't, Graham had his chance. Though... I sat in bed, sheets pulled up to my chin, staring at the doorway. *Why not both*? My wonderful, pre-coffee, meme-driven brain asked. Oz specifically used the word exclusive yesterday. As in, we weren't.

Was that the stupidest thought ever to entertain after how amazing last night was? Maybe. Did that stop me from doing exactly that? Nope.

"Up to you," Oz said. "I won't be offended if you give him five minutes."

"Breakfast?" I offered weakly, not sure what I was asking.

"Can you promise me you won't be thinking about this very moment the entire morning if you don't talk to him?"

fighting for it

I could lie and promise that. But not really, because I was super bad at lying. "I'm here with you."

"If he hadn't pushed you away, would you have gone out with me last night?"

I had no idea if Graham would've been as amicable about Oz as Oz was about him. Though, given Graham's whole *this is for your own good* attitude, probably not. "I would've wanted to."

"If you want to talk to him, talk to him. I won't take it wrong. I meant the things I said yesterday."

I raised my brows as all the things Oz said rushed into my thoughts, carried on his heavy, seductive tone, including the part where he called me a dirty slut—in the best way possible—and said he wanted Graham to watch us fuck.

Great, now there was a throb of desire between my legs, because I'd do that in a heartbeat... after a lot of overthinking.

I climbed from bed and pulled on a T-shirt. "I'll talk to him and then I'm yours again."

Oz wrapped his arms around my waist before I could grab a pair of panties. He crushed his mouth to mine as he slipped a hand between my legs to tease his fingers over my bare, damp skin. He growled against my lips. "You're mine the entire time, but otherwise, I agree."

That shouldn't turn me into a gooey puddle of desire. It totally did. I dressed quickly and opened the door. Graham was still there. I kind of didn't expect that. Would he ask to speak with me alone?

He looked past me, and then met my gaze. "The two of you are just friends?"

"Things have changed." I'd rather do this in front of Oz. He sounded sincere when he said he was fine with it, and I believed him. But I didn't want any misunderstandings later. Besides, he made me feel safe. Not that Graham would hurt me physically, but he had the potential to do a number on my heart. "And yes, he knows what happened—and didn't—between us," I said.

"And he's okay with being your rebound guy?"

I scowled at the phrase.

Graham frowned and shook his head. "I didn't mean that."

"You did," Oz said. "And I'm okay with Luna and I defining our relationship, not you."

I wanted to get this bit over with. Yeah, there was an animalistic appeal in being fought over, but I hated conflict. Especially being at the center of it. "This is why you're here?"

"I'm here to apologize to you, and hopefully talk."

I crossed my arms. The physical barrier was to remind me I wouldn't listen to a weak apology that part of me hoped would be so good I couldn't ignore it.

fighting for it

"When you showed up the other day, when you kissed me..." Graham trailed off and looked past me toward Oz again. "Can we do this outside?" He nodded to the steps next to him.

There it was. I shook my head. "I'm good here, thanks."

Graham sighed. "I *have* missed you. I *was* staying away from you. I figured you'd moved on." His gaze flicked toward Oz again before landing on me. "But I lied when I said I hoped that was the case. I also wanted you to find me."

This wasn't an apology, and it wasn't tugging at all on that spark of hope that I had about anything to do with Graham. At least swooning chibi-Luna was still half asleep.

Why was I talking to Graham at all? I'd barely started things with Oz. Who was also right that I was still thinking about Graham. Damn my optimism that I wouldn't have to give either up. "I don't know what you expect me to say."

"When your pet bear said the things he did, he hit every doubt I'd had when I was your teacher," Graham said. "Touched on very fucking reason I kept my distance."

"This is a crappy apology." I could swoon and daydream from now until eternity, but refused to imagine an *I'm sorry* when there wasn't one.

Graham frowned. "I promise I'm getting there. Cole's accusation reminded me of all the reasons I kept my distance, yes. But when the news hit last night, I couldn't stop worrying about you. Which meant I was thinking about you, about what originally happened, and about all the reasons it was hard for me to not tell you I was attracted to you. I'm sorry for what I said the other day. I shouldn't have put this on you. I do miss you, and I never should've used you as an excuse."

Graham rested a hand on my face and tilted his head.

He was going to kiss me. My pulse roared so loudly in my ears I couldn't hear anything else.

I placed my hand on his chest and stepped to arm's length, breaking his touch. Did I want the kiss? Unfortunately, yes. Did I also kind of want to see what Oz would do? Deck Graham, tell him to stick around and watch while Oz fucked me, or walk out the door without a word?

That last one terrified me. "Thank you for the apology." I kept my voice cool. "Was there something else?" I moved my hand from Graham to the door, ready to shut him out.

"I know how to make this right. How to fix the bad press that story is going to generate."

"How?" Oz asked.

fighting for it

"This has been blowing up all night in the tech and education communities. I've been looking for my own name, and worried you were at home, falling into a panic spiral. I'm glad you were distracted." Graham's voice tilted at an odd timbre.

Oz made a low, frustrated growling sound I felt in the soles of my feet. "Do you ever offer a tl;dr version?" He asked.

"Context is important," Graham said. "Fine. This isn't going away. If it does, it could come back any time, as last night proved, and the only way to prevent that from being an ongoing threat is to deal with it. The world needs to see the real Luna. The kind of infamy you have, your last notable hack defines you. Ten years ago, you brought the world to its knees, and five years ago you saved it. The internet needs to remember the latter."

That was idealistic, even for me. "I didn't actually *save the world*."

"Schools and colleges versus government contractors? To most people, that's saving the world." Graham made it sound simple.

Oz stepped up next to me and settled his hand at the small of my back. "What you're talking about would have to be big, and even then, there's no guarantee it's going to overwrite what's already out there."

"Luna knows people who will help this go viral. Ramsey Miller. Sadie Sews. Grayso—"

"I don't know them." Okay, I knew Ramsey, but I'd met Sadie *once*. She definitely wasn't on the list of people I felt comfortable asking for favors.

"How do *you* know that, Graham?" Oz asked. "How long have you been watching Luna?"

"Violet is surrounded by people who live public lives. If Violet knows them, Luna knows them."

I noticed Graham didn't answer the second question. Did he avoid it on purpose?

"It may not work, but you know how the saying goes—the odds are better than if we don't try." Graham's tone was one of conviction. "The news hit last night, and while it won't vanish quickly it will fade. We don't have to shout louder right this second. As the original story gets softer, over the next week or so, we come in with something stronger."

"And you have the knowledge to make this happen." Oz's tone was flat with disbelief. "Luna can go to Sadie herself. To Grayson. To Ramsey."

The people around Violet really did lead public lives. I'd never thought of that before. But Graham was the right person to help with Graham's idea. Go figure. "It's not just about tossing the information out there and crossing our fingers," I said. "Going viral isn't a science, but there are reproducible elements that increase the odds."

fighting for it

"I never cease to be amazed at how much knowledge you retain." Graham smiled broadly.

Which didn't make me swoon at all. There may have been a rush of heat to my face, but that didn't mean I was enjoying any part of this conversation or wishing in any way that I'd taken more of Graham's other courses.

"Graham teaches how information travels, both behind the scenes and right in front of our faces." I hadn't taken the more advanced courses on The Psychology of Social Media, but I was in as many Gen Ed ones as I was allowed to cram into my schedule without disrupting my Pre Reqs. "One of his final projects"—for the course I couldn't get into—"was to create a piece of media and make it go viral."

Number of views were part of the grade, but just as important was how each element was utilized.

"I've learned a lot from seeing people do this over and over," Graham said.

Oz's cough was exaggerated. "In other words, you've made a habit of letting your students do the work, and you reaping the benefits."

I wouldn't say a felony conviction was a benefit of helping me.

"You never learned from the people you worked with? Who work for you? What a sad life that must be." Graham's derision was almost tangible. "Every student in that course has lifetime access to every project. The data, the theories, the execution. I don't hoard information. Would you like a list of references of what my students have gone on to do, using the things I taught them? I guarantee you'll know their names. I also guarantee none of them leaves the kind of impression Luna does."

He was exaggerating, or everyone who'd ever met me would feel that way. My flush deepened anyway, running from my toes to the roots of my hair.

"This isn't my decision," Oz said.

Graham's idea was solid, and he was right. This wasn't going away. Someone would always know—always want to talk about—what I did ten years ago. I didn't like to think of myself as infamous, but I'd have to be blind to not see my own legacy. Every job interview where someone said *Aren't you the girl….* Cases like last night, where someone like Scott McAllister recognized my name.

I needed to get ahead of things now, and Graham had the skills to help me do that.

"Luna." Oz's voice softened. "This is your future. Decide what to do next for you. Not for me or Graham or anyone else."

I didn't make decisions without considering the people around me.

"Imagine the challenge," Graham said.

"That was what got me in trouble in the first place." And a huge part of the reason I had to consider how it would impact my friends. But, *sigh,* the challenge of making this work—of doing it perfectly—really spoke to me.

Graham reached for me, then dropped his hand. "There are no dark or light powers, no matter what books and movies say. There's only what you choose to use your gifts for, and this is a good cause—you're a good cause."

I wouldn't describe myself that way, but what he was proposing was a good idea. And damn it, I did want to be challenged. Laying cable was a nice distraction, but digital penetration… "Let's do it. Where and when do we start?"

"The sooner the better." Graham looked at Oz. "My plan was to buy you breakfast."

I prayed Oz meant everything he said, about being fine with whatever I decided. I didn't want to lose or have to resent him because of this. I wasn't going to test those limits too much today. "I have plans this morning."

"Luna. A moment?"

I didn't know what to make of Oz's flat tone, and I didn't like the crevice of doubt it sent slicing through me.

Chapter Eight

I'd spent the last three years spinning my wheels and never getting traction. With work. With relationships.

And in less than forty-eight hours, everything was ramping up like someone had quadrupled the number of threads on the system that was my life.

It wasn't possible to move too far away from Graham in my apartment, but Oz and I did step out of ear reach.

"Last night was about getting you back on your feet," Oz said softly. "What he's proposing—will it help?"

I shrugged. "It's the only idea I have. It's also a really good idea. I also want you there—I want your input." The longer I thought about it, the more this entire thing felt reasonable.

"Do it. You and I have time."

"I hope so."

Oz tilted my head up with a finger under my chin and brushed his thumb over my lips. "Bring an overnight bag and come to my place after."

fighting for it

"Okay." Heat flooded me on a wave of happiness. I turned to Graham. "Let's do it."

We agreed on a place, and Oz told Graham we'd meet him there.

It'd be nice to take a shower, but mine was barely big enough for me. Oz and I finished dressing—which unfortunately meant he put his shirt on—and were on our way.

Oz kept his hand on my thigh when he wasn't shifting gears.

I texted Violet with a promise to call later. Or tomorrow. I wasn't sure yet. I checked my email, too, to make sure I didn't have any requests for interviews waiting.

There were already two replies to the resumes I'd sent out yesterday. Both said *We're not interested at this time.* They didn't even offer to keep my resume on file. Rude.

Graham was waiting when we arrived. He'd grabbed us a booth in the far corner of the restaurant—one of those that was a single half-circle wrapped around a table.

Oz slid in next to Graham and pulled me to sit next to him, sandwiching Oz in the middle.

Graham didn't look pleased as he put an extra foot between them.

We placed our orders, and Graham told the waitress to leave the coffee pot and expect that we'd need more. Was it bad that I liked that throwback to the old days, when we'd be in a random twenty-four-hour diner, talking code strategies until three in the morning and downing *way* too much caffeine?

"The basics." Graham pulled a leather portfolio from the seat next to him and opened it on the table to a blank notebook page. "This isn't just about getting Luna's name out there; we have to be smart about the details. Nailing the SEO. Ensuring the right click throughs…" As he talked, he wrote out neat columns across the top of the page.

So. Many. Schoolgirl flashbacks.

"How is this different than every other person out there who does the same and never gets seen?" Oz asked.

I knew this one, and the answer was so simple it didn't sound like a real reply. "Because we don't do it the same as every other person out there."

Oz raised an eyebrow and stared me down with amused disbelief.

Wowza that heated gaze made me squirm.

"It's like playing Street Fighter 2." Graham's voice held an edge. "Everyone knows that Abel's Infinite exists. The combo is programmed in. But it takes a whole new level of skill to hit the right buttons, under pressure, on purpose."

"And you can hit the right buttons," Oz said with disbelief.

fighting for it

Graham looked past him, to hold my gaze. "Every time."

Was he flirting with me? With my date…boyfriend? Bodyguard? … sitting between us?

Oz coughed to clear his throat.

Graham sank into his seat, but not before I caught his smirk. "In reality? I suck at Street Fighter. For the purposes of this analogy? Yes. I know how to lay out a web of the kind of genuine, interconnected links that search engines love. Every time someone searches for Luna's name, whether they want to know about the stuff we got in trouble for or see pictures of her sucking cock, our good results pop up first."

Was my face bright red? It had to be. Especially since I was fantasizing about Graham taking pictures while I sucked Oz's cock. Geez. "No one's searching for my name like that." My voice came out thicker than I intended.

"He's right." Oz nodded at my phone. "Look for yourself."

I pulled up a search app and typed my name in. There it was—*Luna Murphy suck cock* plain as day in the auto-complete suggestions. "Why…? Never mind." I was a woman in tech who just became a minor celebrity. It was tempting to see what kind of results the phrase returned, but I swiped away.

Another email came in, and I couldn't help but glance at the message from another company I'd sent my resume to yesterday. *We're sorry to inform you...*

My heart sank at another rejection, and I set my phone aside. "So… SEO. Click throughs. How do we make it happen?"

The waitress returned with three full coffee cups, two silver pots, and a bowl full of plain and flavored creamers.

"Keywords are great, but on a really simplistic level, other people talking about you, using those keywords, is the best. That's where your friends come in." Graham grabbed three French vanilla and dumped them into his coffee. "They're going to give us the kind of web that most companies pay huge money to build, with their existing networks."

I went straight for the sugar. Plain cream. "They're not my friends. I barely know them."

"I suspect you've left an impression. Oz has connections too, if he's willing to use them."

"Without question." Oz might look like a black coffee kind of guy, but he loaded up on as much sugar as I did.

Graham wrote out more notes on his pad. "You were at Rinslet when they were Cord. You know the original gang. Jordan has a huge fanbase."

Oz nodded. "I do and he does."

"Judith—"

fighting for it

"No." Oz clipped the word off. He exhaled slowly, nostrils flared. "This isn't her area of expertise."

I was asking him about that reaction later for sure.

"Why are you doing this, Oz?" Graham asked. "You were *just a friend* two nights ago, and now you're all in, for whatever Luna needs."

I downed my coffee too fast, ignoring that it scalded the roof of my mouth. I was going to need the extra energy if the tension between the two of them kept up.

Oz refilled my cup. "Fucking her didn't flip a switch. I was all-in before, too. Why did *you* show up this morning?"

"This is my fault. I need to make it right." Graham dropped his pen with a soft clatter.

Say what? "How could you *possibly* arrive at that conclusion?"

"When you hit my classroom, I was in my second year as a full-time professor, and my bosses were watching me very closely. I—" Graham sighed. "I was sleeping with the Dean of Computer Science's son when I was a TA."

"Imagine that." Enter Oz: Deadpan mode.

Graham shot him a glare. "He wasn't my student, but when we broke up, it brought a lot of extra scrutiny down on me. And then I met Luna."

He turned to me. "And the first time I heard you dive into a topic you were passionate about, I knew I was fucked. Tiff had been a good friend—I thought—for a long time. I asked her to act as a kind of buffer. She wasn't supposed to fuck you. Especially not the way she did."

That was a lot to process. "I had no idea you knew her. You never said… Why didn't you ever tell me the two of you were friends?"

"Biggest reason, I was trying to keep my distance from you. I had no idea who she really was."

"And you never looked into her." Oz's *yeah, right*, was implied.

Graham shook his head. "That wasn't something I did with my friends. Especially in those days. Do you?"

I did. It had taken a lot of restraint on my part to not go full stalker on Oz. I came close a few times, but as long as I didn't have to crack any databases to get the information, it was considered public, and fair game, right? *Sigh*. Yeah, okay, I may have crossed a line or two.

But I wasn't in the habit of doing things like that when I started college, and while I didn't like that Graham never told me he knew Tiff, his reasons made sense

"You've got some sort of knight-with-a-tarnished-soul complex," Oz said.

fighting for it

"And you are…?" Graham asked. The waitress arrived, and he took plates from her, setting them in front of the right people.

Oz dumped a notable amount of hot sauce on his hash browns. "No tarnish here. I'm infatuated with an incredible mind and body, and the woman made up of it all, and I want to see her succeed."

Violet would tell me no one was Oz's level of kind and adoring without wanting something in return, but I was. I didn't do nice things on barter. Did that make me naive and get me in trouble?

Sometimes. Tiff was a great example. Was I happier with my decisions, regardless? With seeing the genuine and good in people? Without question.

I also wanted to keep this conversation on track. It seemed every time we swerved just a little, the guys slammed into each other's guard rails. I grabbed my phone to make notes of my own, and frowned at three more emails telling me *thanks but no thanks* to my resume. That was six total out of fifteen, all rejected before ten in the morning. That couldn't be good.

Nothing to do for it but move forward. "Next steps in this plan. What do I need to do?"

"You talk to every person you know, or who's connected to someone you know, who has a public presence. You ask for airtime, especially if they have a big social media following." Graham made it sound easy.

It couldn't possibly be. "What do I talk to them about?"

"Yourself. Whatever you'd like. Whatever they ask you. You can focus on what you did five years ago, creating a patch for the malware, if you'd like, but mostly talk about what you enjoy doing in your free time. Who you are."

Uh…yawn? "No one wants to hear that."

"I hate to say it, but I think he's onto something." Oz's demeanor changed in an instant. It was subtle, but I was skilled at seeing stoic lighten into reserved.

"I need a script, or a primer, or something." I babbled when I was under pressure. Or froze. Which would be worse?

"You really don't," Graham said.

Oz squeezed my knee. "You'll shine, no matter what."

I didn't see what they saw but arguing wasn't getting me anywhere. "It can't be as simple as getting on a few podcasts and livestreams."

"It's not," Graham said. "But that's your next step. Get on people's schedules, the sooner the better. While you're doing that, I'll put the framework in place to tie everything up. The SEO. The URL's.

fighting for it

Send me your schedule as you have it, and then we'll move to the next steps."

"Which are…?" Oz prompted.

Graham waved a hand. "Programming. Luna and I have it."

"I'll help." Oz wasn't asking.

"No offense—"

"Plenty meant, I'm sure." Oz's words were abrasive, but his tone and posture were still more casual. "I know my shit as well as you do, old man."

Graham scoffed. "You're seriously calling me old."

"I'm doing it facetiously. Who made an arcade reference in his analogy?"

"And who understood it?" Graham countered.

Was this where they'd finally come to blows? Was being watched over by two sexy, brainy men worth it if they were constantly threatening to fight?

Oz's chuckle caught me off-guard. "Guilty as charged," he said.

Did chest thumping just become bonding? Was that hot or a bit too caveman for me? I shouldn't be so fuzzy on the answer.

"If you've kept your skills fresh, we could use your help." Graham worked his jaw. "If you can follow directions." He seemed to add as an afterthought.

"Directions, yes. Orders not so much," Oz said.

"Big surprise there." Graham's tone was still light.

I liked the lighter mood, regardless of the testosterone-fueled lead-in. My phone rang, and I grabbed it. An interview? Maybe? I hit *Answer* before I registered that it was my Landlord's name on my screen.

"Hello." I kept my tone sweet, pretending I hadn't been mostly avoiding him.

"Luna. I was surprised to see your name in the news this morning." He wasn't nearly as friendly. "You're a convicted felon."

Frack. "I'm not. It was reduced to a misdemeanor, and even that's been removed from my record now."

"Now. You didn't disclose it when you filled out your application."

"You didn't ask." Was I wrong? Had he?

Oz held out his hand. "Give me the phone," he said softly.

"Look, you're consistently late on your rent, and now I find out you're a criminal. You have until the end of the month to get out."

What? All the coffee I'd had sank like a stone in my stomach. "You're evicting me?"

"I am. End of the month." He disconnected.

fighting for it

And now I was going to be homeless in three weeks. I dropped my phone on the table and my head into my hands as I sank in my seat.

"Did I just…" Oz was a man of few words, but not a man who was usually at a loss for words. "Did he kick you out for having a record?"

I nodded.

"He can't do that."

Graham sucked in a sharp breath through his teeth. "Actually…"

"Of course you'd know that." Oz sigh-growled. "Give me his name, I'll make this right."

I covered my phone without looking up, and slid it closer to me. "No." My other hand muffled my voice. Could I let Oz fight it? Call Violet and ask Ramsey to do something? Yes.

Was it worth the stress, to stay in a place where I wasn't wanted, and where friction and distrust had been building for months because I was late *a lot* with my rent?

No.

"Luna." Oz's voice was tight.

I finally looked at him. "Let it go." *Please.* I wouldn't ask, as much as I wanted to soften the request. He needed to know I meant this.

Chapter Nine

Graham cleared his throat loudly and the people two tables over shot him a glare.

I wanted to sink into my seat and hide forever. It wasn't so much the embarrassment factor as it was the cloud of tension that had been growing since Graham showed up this morning. The sun had just started to peek through that gray haze, and now the warmth was gone again.

"This just became mission critical," Graham said.

"Agreed." Oz clipped off the word.

The one thing they consistently agreed on was helping me. It was a starting point. "Graham said it would take a few weeks. This isn't something you can force."

"We can make some things happen faster. This is going to take more than an hour or two of coffee to plan though." Graham reached for the check.

Oz grabbed it first. "If you don't mind the drive, I have a good setup for that at my place. We can sit on the deck and get some sunshine."

fighting for it

I loved that idea. Oz's yard ran into the mountains and it was gorgeous up there. Besides, there was barely room for two of us in my place, and from what I'd seen of Graham's, it wasn't much bigger. "Okay."

"Jeremy Ranch?" Graham raised an eyebrow. "I guess it's not as far away as some things."

How did he know— Because despite telling me he wasn't interested, he'd looked into Oz. I would've if our roles had been reversed.

Oz didn't look impressed. "Does that mean you don't need my address?"

"You'd probably better write it down so I have it." Graham slid his notepad to Oz.

We had our leftovers boxed to go, and Oz paid the bill, despite another protest from Graham.

Oz took me by my place again, to grab my laptop. The computer was a Christmas gift from Hunter, and was spec'd out perfectly for the kind of coding I did. The nicest things I owned were from Violet and her guys, and I was forbidden from protesting because they were gifts. I loved the consideration behind them.

I jumped in the shower for the fastest rinse off in history, tugged on a yellow sundress that was perfect for summer mountain weather, and I was in Oz's truck again in under five minutes.

He leaned in and dragged his nose up my neck, both tickling and enticing. "You smell like Luna again."

"I assume that's a good thing."

"For now. We'll have to change that later when work is done."

Chibi Luna whimpered in my head, and it was possible my own tiny squeak slipped out.

Oz stole a kiss that was far hotter than it should've been considering it lasted half a second, and we were on our way to his place again.

As much as I wanted to sink into the simplicity of his hand on my thigh and the gorgeous drive up the mountains, the morning had raised a lot of questions, and as many were for Oz as Graham.

"Who's Dorothy?" My question popped out on its own, without any fanfare.

Oz glanced at me. "Ah."

That wasn't an answer. It didn't even mean anything. "Why did you shut Graham down when he mentioned Judith? Why are you really doing this—"

"Luna—"

"Do *not* give me the tl;dr versions of anything. I need context."

"Hmm." Oz downshifted as we hit the first steep grade up of our trip. "When we worked for Cord, when it was still young—when—we were, Scott and Zach went out of their way to bring in

fighting for it

young, undiscovered talent. Most of us had never worked anywhere but McDonalds or bagging groceries. We certainly had no idea what a real corporate environment was like. And we were living our dreams."

I had no idea what this had to do with my questions, but I'd asked for context, so I was willing to wait through more talking than I usually heard from Oz in a full day. Plus, I enjoyed the sound of his voice and devoured any story I could about *back in the day*.

"Judith is Dorothy. I'm Oz, I used to call her Judy, it's—"

"A roundabout reference to Judy Garland, I get it." This wasn't nearly as scandalous as an emotional reaction from Oz implied it would be. I was relieved.

"She's the reason I was at the party last night, and never call her Judy, she hates it."

Okay, industry friends, then. Or... frenemies? Judith was polite. Friendly.

"She's my ex-wife," Oz said.

What in the what? The emotions that washed over me were muddied and dense. It wasn't like I thought Oz was a virginal saint, especially after last night, but we'd gone to a party at his ex-wife's behest? I didn't have a right to be jealous, but I was feeling something I didn't like.

He glanced over and squeezed my leg. "I'm assuming you still want context?"

"Uh... duh?"

"Don't make any assumptions until I get to the end."

Too late. "No more than I already have."

He shrugged. "Fair. All of us at Cord were also fucking around a lot. Pairing off. Grouping off. Even those of us who were *together* were openly sleeping with other people. It was all consensual. Not like what Violet has, because it wasn't closed up all nice and neat. The fucking was fun, but the flexibility of loving multiple people was what I liked. I'm not monogamous."

"You're polyamorous." Look at me, putting pieces together like a genius or something.

He nodded. "You deserve to know early on. I wasn't planning to keep it from you, but I had hoped the circumstances would be a little less... crammed in the middle of everything else."

This was where the jealousy should surge, wasn't it? Why was I assured instead? "Are you seeing other people now?"

"No."

"Will you want to?"

"Don't know. You've raised the bar on what I like in a person. I've been hooked on you for a while now."

fighting for it

I'd been drooling over him for ages, but that didn't stop me from looking other places. Like Graham. Not that what I had with Graham was anything more than obsession at this point. I didn't know what to do with this information. "Is that why you got divorced? Jealousy?"

"No." Oz's answer came without hesitation. "We had a difference in opinion about priorities, and in the end, she chose her career."

Ouch. "I'm sorry."

"It's fine." He sounded like he meant it and radiated the same sincerity. "This isn't a wicked ex story. I hated it at the time, but it's been more than a decade and the distance has given me time to appreciate her friendship, without the romantic attachment."

He made it sound simple. Except for the *more than a decade* part. I'd barely been legal for more than a decade. "Okay."

"*Okay?*" Oz echoed. "Did I break you?" Teasing slid into his question.

The lighter tone helped unstick my brain. "It's a lot to process, and it's not about tech. Not directly, anyway. People are more complicated than software, and I don't know what's expected of me in this situation."

"Don't think about it like that. I'm telling you so that you know, not to trick you or see how you respond. Though, I obviously hope you're okay with the entire thing."

"I think I am." Wasn't I? Logically, these should be warning flags. My new boyfriend—I liked the sound of *Oz is my boyfriend*—had a past of fucking his co-workers and was still friends with his ex-wife. But I didn't feel the issue. I wasn't concerned about it meaning bad things for us.

Maybe he should be the one concerned, because now I was wondering more than ever if I could have at least one night with both him and Graham.

The tiny lines Oz traced along my thigh with his thumb were comforting. "I do the apprenticeships, I rent out the inexpensive housing, because when I was in my early twenties someone gave me an amazing chance, and others deserve the same," he said. "You... You're this brilliant mind capable of so much. If you were ten years older, you'd have been one of the original crew. I'm glad you weren't, for your sake. You have access to so much more tech. Diversity. Freedom. But if anyone deserves a chance, it's you."

That stunned me to silence. And made me blush, I was sure. And was without a doubt, hotter than anything I'd ever fantasized about Oz saying to me.

"Besides," he said. Your intelligence is really fucking sexy, and *God* I love fucking you."

fighting for it

That was pretty hot too. "We have so much in common."

He chuckled. "Any other questions? I'll answer them all."

"I'm good for now." Really good. I could even ignore that my career was about to once again be over before it started. But that wouldn't be an issue, because we were going to fix things.

"Good."

We chatted about little things on the rest of the trip. He'd left messages for a few contacts while I was in my apartment. I sent Violet a text and asked her for the same.

We reached Oz's place, and Graham arrived a few minutes later. It was cooler up here, given we were in the mountains, but the sun was high enough to strike my face and warm my skin.

"We should do this on the lawn, out back." Where I could see the little blue wildflowers and dandelions along the edges of the grass, that had significantly increased in number since I mentioned I liked them.

"We'll get glare on the screens," Oz said.

I shouldn't be out in the sun too much anyway. I'd burn. "We'll go inside when that happens. Or do you want me to beg?" I turned innocent eyes on Oz.

"So very desperately." Oz's voice dropped an octave.

Graham did that loud throat clearing thing.

I'll beg you, too. The offer died in my throat. Fantasy, meet the reality of rejection. Apparently none of Graham's actions or apology had erased that burning moment of humiliation from my mind. Go figure.

The tension flowing freely between Oz and Graham didn't help. The feeling had lightened in the diner, but the drive seemed to be enough to restore it to its original, thought-clogging heaviness.

"I'll grab a blanket," Oz said. "Give Graham the mini-tour and pick a spot outside."

I nodded. Impulse wanted to reach for Graham's hand, and tug him through the main floor of the house. What good was an impulse if over-thinking stopped it before it started? "This way." I jerked my thumb toward the rear of the house instead.

As Graham and I headed toward the yard, I pointed out the important things. "Bathroom's down the hall. Help yourself to anything in the fridge. Glasses are in the cupboard to the right of the sink." Oz gave me the tour once, and it had stuck in my head. It was terse but welcoming. I was still impressed he managed to pull off the combination.

We headed onto the deck. "Pick a chair. Power's there." I pointed to the outlets at the back of the house.

fighting for it

"You know your way around." Graham's tone was off.

He didn't get to be jealous. He'd pushed me away. Still, I didn't want him to not like Oz. I also wanted him to still want me.

"Everyone still dressed?" Oz called as he joined us on the deck.

Graham scowled. "You asked Luna to show me around and she did. The fuck kind of comment is that?"

The tension was back, hurrah. I stepped between the men, not because I thought they might come to blows, but it felt appropriate to physically divide them.

"If you're going to keep poking and prodding each other for a reaction, I'm not going to do this." I wouldn't. I couldn't. "You're supposed to be the adults here. Act like it."

Chapter Ten

"You're an adult, too." Graham's retort was tinged with frustration.

"In fact, you might be too old for him." Oz added.

I glared at Oz. "I'm not working with the two of you if you can't get along." They were going to suffocate me with resentment and distaste, especially since I was the focal point for them coming together.

"I'm fine with him." Oz shrugged.

Graham shook his head. "You keep saying that, but—"

"Enough." I wanted them both here, but we had to do something about the friction. I grabbed my deck from my bag, and left the rest of my things on the deck. They both knew I read tarot, though I'd never done it around them. "Leave your laptops here. We're going to ask the cards what it will take for the two of you to get along."

"I—" Graham stopped when I looked at him, and he set his laptop bag on the patio table. "Sure."

I understood that most people thought me consulting tarot cards was hokey at best and out right stupid at the other end of the spectrum. Oz and Graham had always accepted me. It was one of the reasons I adored both of them. Wanted to spend time with them.

Oz lay a large blanket on the back lawn.

I knelt on one side and gestured for them to take spots opposite me.

"How does this work?" There was no judgment in Graham's question, only curiosity. He sat with one knee to his chest, and the other leg stretched out.

I slid the deck into my hands and held it. What was I looking for? I wanted to resolve the conflict between Graham and Oz.

"On a really basic level, cards are drawn with a specific question in mind. Without that, the answers can lead to more confusion. Sometimes it's one card, and other times it's a layout meant to answer a specific type of situation." In this case, a single card wouldn't do, but I had a spread in mind that would help guide us.

Oz's legs were stretched in front of him and he leaned his weight on his wrists behind him. "And the spirits guide your hands?"

"Some people read that way, yes. I see it as the randomness of the universe giving me a little extra insight when I'm struggling to find my own." I shuffled the deck three times, then cut it.

"You look for advice in chaos theory?" Graham asked.

I repeated the main question in my head. *How do we resolve this conflict?* "That's as valid an approach as any."

Oz nodded. "I like it."

I laid seven cards out, four in a square and three more to the right, including an extra on one of the questions, to apply specifically to each man. Since they'd never seen this before, I would explain a little more in depth than normal.

I pointed to the first card, a Seven of Swords. "This one asks what's at the root of the conflict."

"And it's upside down, so that means bad, right?" Graham asked.

"It means the inverse of the card's original meaning."

Oz leaned in, studying the layout. "Like Bizarro Superman?"

"More or less." I was pleased they were showing interest and not just sitting there sullenly. I hated being placated, and neither of them gave off that vibe. "This one is about deception. Secret plans. And when it's reversed, it has to do with being hasty or impulsive when it comes to how we think." The meaning of the card flitted through my thoughts, swirling into how it applied to our situation. "Tiff tricking me ten years ago." My voice trailed off.

fighting for it

I knew my mistake was at the core of all of this, but I didn't appreciate the universe calling me out like that on step one.

"That feels deceptively simple," Oz said.

"Sometimes it works that way, and others it's not so direct." I pointed to the Six of Swords in the second spot. "This is what we can do to help resolve the conflict." A sigh rolled through me. "We need to focus on healing and moving away from the churn. You two need to understand that I brought this on myself. I was manipulated into it. Stop putting it on Graham." That was a stretch of the core meaning, but that was what they had to do in order to move on. "You can't change what happened, but we can repair it."

"Do you have every one of those memorized?" Graham sounded impressed. "That's amazing."

The compliment made me flush in the rising sunshine. "It's taken years of practice." I pointed to the next card. "This question is where is the clash in your perspectives coming from?"

"That one doesn't look like the others. It's an important one, right?" Oz asked.

Most people treated this like a party trick. The fact that both men were asking genuine questions warmed me. "Major Arcana, and yes. This is The World. It's a happy ending after a rough journey."

"There's no conflict in perspective there." Graham focused on me. "Who doesn't want a happily ever after?"

"The issue isn't wanting it, it's that you see each other as an obstacle to achieving it," I said.

Oz looked thoughtful. "That's true."

The next card, the Queen of Swords reversed, glared at me, accusingly. "Which leads us to what my role is in that conflict. You're letting your feelings for me drive you to bitterness, vindication, malice, and pessimism." The words hurt.

"What's wrong?" Graham asked.

I didn't want to be a catalyst for those things. "Introspection hurts sometimes." But that was why we were doing this, wasn't it? To move past the hurt.

"That one looks more positive." Oz pointed to the Ten of Coins. "It feels like success."

It was. "That card says what you should keep in mind as you work with Graham. It's hard-earned accomplishment after a difficult venture."

Graham snorted. The first derisive sound I'd heard from him since we started.

I didn't blame him in this case. "Cole has those things. Graham has been cut off from them, but that doesn't stop him from wanting the same."

"Which is reasonable." Graham sounded defensive. "I haven't exactly been a slacker in life."

fighting for it

"It's totally reasonable." I focused on Oz. "Imagine you were in his shoes. You'd decided to help the wrong person, and it cost you the future you'd built for yourself. You wouldn't begrudge him that, would you?"

Oz clenched his jaw. "You're not the wrong person."

"If I'm not wrong for you, I wasn't for Graham, either." I didn't realize that could be taken a couple ways until the words crossed my lips, but I wasn't going to clarify. "Speaking of..." I looked at Graham, and gestured at the Three of Wands reversed. "You've worked hard, and been on a tremendous journey, without having to leave home. Now that your probation is over, you see the things you worked for, the things you wanted, and you can't reach them. At the same time, Oz has a lot of them. Don't hold that against him."

"I can't just flip a switch and change the way I feel," Graham said.

"No, but you can make a conscious effort to see things from each other's perspectives." I studied the last card—the Queen of Cups, and mentally dragged in a deep breath. "You're both here because you say you want to help me. You need to work together." How could I phrase this? "If you trust me—my thoughts, my intuition—then you need to trust that I'm okay with both of you."

Oz hovered his fingers over the cards, never making contact. "You make it sound simple."

"I know it's not." I looked over the spread one last time before gathering the cards and tucking them away again.

I needed to call Violet, if we were going to be here for a while. Let her know I was all right, Oz was amazing, and that I needed a favor or two. I wandered away from the blanket as I pulled up her number, but not so far that Oz and Graham were out of sight.

The tarot card reading was insightful, but that didn't mean I trusted them to play nice.

"Hey, Lucky Lady." Violet was cheerful. "Did Cole untie you long enough to say *hi*?"

Would he tie me up? Probably so if I begged. *Wowza, that* was hot. I stashed the fantasy for future reference. "More or less. I got your text. Wanted to check in. And I need a favor."

"Anything. What's up?"

"I need to talk to Sadie. Grayson. See if I can be on their shows. Maybe Hunter can hook me up with people who want to interview me."

"Whoa." Violet's tone shifted to serious. "Yank the reins, L. Second of all, you're going to need to back up and tell me why, but first, you can't just do that. You can't launch into random requests, and pretend you didn't have that bear of a man you adore in your apartment overnight. You're still with him, aren't you?"

I looked over at Oz to see him staring back. Geez, I liked the way he looked at me. "Oz and Graham both."

"Uh, what?" Violet sounded amused. "You owe me so many details. What kind of story is there? A juicy one."

"No."

"Not yet, you mean."

This wasn't what Violet was implying, no matter how much I wanted otherwise.

"How was it? How was he?" Violet asked. "Them?"

"Just him." I was intently aware of Graham's gaze on me too. It wouldn't be hard to guess what I was talking about, even with only half the conversation. "And amazing." I didn't want to discourage Graham, but I wasn't going to hide that away for his benefit.

"Details when you don't have an audience. Or at least, more detailed impressions," Violet said. "Why do you want to be on Sadie's channel?"

I gave her a brief rundown of what Graham proposed and how we were approaching it.

"Everyone is going to be watching you, if you do this," Violet's teasing had melted to concern.

"You can't do some things in public and not all of them."

"You do."

She sighed. "True, but there's still a lot more of our lives out there than you're going to be comfortable with when it's you." One of her boyfriends, Ramsey, had been in politics, and still loved the spotlight. That meant she and Hunter caught the edges of it as well.

"My name is already out there. This way, I can control the narrative."

Violet *tsked*.

I rolled my eyes. "I know, I can't completely control it, but I can drive some of it." I had to believe that. "I've already been evicted over it." I hadn't meant to let that slip.

"No, L. It's okay. We have a guest room, and you're always welcome here."

I didn't know what I was going to do about the apartment situation, but I wasn't going to be comfortable living with Violet's guys. I liked them fine, but I wasn't close with them like I was her. "Can I let you know?"

She sighed. "Okay. I'll talk to people and get back to you. Do you want them to go through me, or call you directly?"

I'd much rather they go through Violet, but she'd take it on herself to become my *assistant* in this, and the last thing she needed was me piling more work on her. She did that just fine on her own. "Send them directly to me," I said. This was my project, and I needed to dive in headfirst. Hiding in the shadows except during interview time would only make the task more difficult. "And thank you."

"Always," Violet said.

We chatted for another minute or so before disconnecting, and I rejoined Oz and Graham on the blanket.

"Stay in one of my apartments," Oz said.

I shook my head. That was as bad as intruding in Violet's life. "That's how you make your money, and right now, I can't afford any place you rent." Not that he was running high-end condos, but I barely had the couple hundred a month for my tiny studio.

"I'm not going to miss it for a single unit, I promise. I'd offer to pay for your new place instead, but you wouldn't take that."

I shook my head. "No. I wouldn't."

"Then it's settled. We'll move you when you're ready."

I didn't remember saying *yes*, but it was one less thing I'd need to worry about now.

"I wouldn't have minded if you shared details." Oz settled a hand on my thigh.

Warmth seared through me at the touch and the light shift in topic. "I shared enough."

"I wouldn't mind details either." Graham's statement caught me off-guard. Before I could ask him if he was serious, he shook his head. "Did you see this new rendering algorithm they're hyping from EdgeBite?"

I could be disappointed at the rapid change in subject or I could be delighted that Graham wanted to talk about the same tech that caught my eye a few days ago. "Yes. The applications are so numerous."

"I'm sorry, did your bear just roll his eyes at me?" Graham looked at Oz with disbelief.

Oz's growl reinforced the nickname. "If you're going to call me anything, G-man, call me Daddy."

I wrinkled my nose in distaste.

"No?" Oz sounded surprised.

"*Daddy* isn't going to work for me." I didn't care what kind of nicknames other people tossed around, but that one didn't float my boat or tickle my pickle.

Oz shrugged. "What do you prefer? I've never cared for *Sir* as a general idea."

Possibly for similar reasons. "I already call you *Oz*." And while it wasn't a nickname I'd given him, I was about the only person who used it.

"You're a wizard?" Graham asked in disbelief.

Oz wiggled his hand. "I've got magic fingers."

Yeah, he did.

fighting for it

"And a magic wand, I assume?" Graham might be skeptical, but the antagonism that had been in his voice earlier was gone. His tone was sliding closer to the teasing he and I shared. "Because Oz wasn't that kind of wizard. Lupin, on the other hand…"

Oz raised an eyebrow. "Werewolf. Buffy. Fucking an adorable redheaded genius. I get it." He connected the barely-related dots in a way most people would puzzle at.

Graham looked as pleased as I was. Did Oz just slide into our *all things fictional are related* game without hesitation?

There was one problem with this whole line of conversation, though. "*Lupin* doesn't really roll off the tongue in the heat of the moment."

"I didn't roll off your tongue last night either," Oz said. "It was more of a lodged in your throat—"

"Seriously?" Graham's amusement faded.

"Definitely not." Oz studied him. "Especially not for you."

Graham furrowed his brow. "What?"

The play on words, on names, was a reach, but not a long one given we'd already edged into Harry Potter territory. I knew where Oz was going with the statement. "Sirius Black was a noble protector. I could see that in Graham."

"And he sacrificed himself." Graham was caught up.

Oz rolled his eyes again. "And he spent a lot of his life before that having fun and playing pranks. Graham doesn't strike me as a *prank* kind of guy. Besides, you're more of a Ravenclaw."

Graham scoffed. "I'm a Gryffindor if I'm anything."

I wasn't. Not even close. Like my not-quite-namesake, "You don't want to hang out with me in Ravenclaw?" I extended my lower lip in an exaggerated pout.

"You're not a Gryffindor. You picked knowledge over good," Oz said.

"I picked Luna."

Heat flooded me at Graham's simple statement. "You're implying that back then, when I came to you with the project, you would've said yes, even if I'd been asking for help debugging a basic Python routine?"

Graham searched my face. "The question is irrelevant. If you'd been asking for help with anything less than what you came to me with, you wouldn't be the you I'd pick."

And now I must be bright red.

Graham turned his attention to Oz. "I notice you didn't sort yourself. Are you going to claim you're a Hufflepuff?"

"Never got my Hogwarts letter." Oz made the answer sound obvious. "I was forced to become a

fighting for it

hedge witch and whore myself out to grow my magic."

"Crossover alert." In the best possible way. I'd enjoyed this with Graham, but with Oz added to the mix, it was a whole new flavor of delightful.

"But a logical one." Graham was already weaving the two worlds in his head. I could practically see those sexy brain gears whirring. "In the UK, they find these magicians young and train them. But after the issues with Grindelwald in the US, revealing magic to so many people at once, the American Ministry locked down. They were more careful about how they approached wizards and witches."

"You've put a lot of thought into this." If Oz wasn't careful, he might start exhibiting distinct emotions beyond *grr* and *hmm*.

"And you haven't?" I asked playfully.

Oz's expression was stoic, but one corner of his mouth tugged up. "I haven't done an in depth analysis of whether or not Harry Potter and The Magicians take place in the same universe, no."

"Do you want to? Because we can go all night, and it's a lot of fun." And now my mind was tripping over all the things we could spend all night doing, and most of them involved fewer clothes, and far more tangible *magic wands*.

When Oz opened his mouth, I was certain he'd say *no*. His, "It's tempting," was a glorious surprise. "But we're not shipping Elliot with Draco."

I wrinkled my nose in distaste.

Graham looked horrified. "Elliot and Quentin forever."

"Finally something else we agree on," Oz said.

I was grinning like a loon. "I knew the two of you had more in common than me."

"We both have good taste. That's obvious." Graham was watching me with those dark eyes again. "You're proof of that."

"Again, I can't argue." Oz's phone rang, and he glanced at the screen. "I need to take this." Like that, he was unreadable again.

I wanted to yank him back as he walked away. I wasn't ready to surrender this moment.

Chapter Eleven

Oz stepped away to take what sounded like a friendly, let's-catch-up call with Jordan.

Probably time to get to work. "We need our laptops for this step?" I started to stand.

"Wait." Graham grabbed my fingertips.

It was a light touch, without assumption or command, but it stalled me. "What's up?"

"A moment of just your time?"

I nodded and sank back to my knees. Disappointment flitted inside when Graham let go of me.

"You seem happy with Oz. Already," Graham said.

You'd make me happy too. I didn't know how to say that without things getting convoluted. How did people propose things like that? *Yeah, I'm seeing the guy, but he and I are both cool with me seeing you, too.* It sounded simple enough, but would Graham accept it?

He might accept it more than the long silence I'd just let stretch between us.

"Right." Graham gave a brief shake of his head. "I'm sorry about what happened the other day. The things I said in the coffee shop. I realize I said the same this morning, but I want you to know that even when there's not an audience, I still mean it. And I'm sorry for what happened back then."

He was still apologizing for the malware debacle. *Sigh.*

"I made those decisions, to do the coding job." I wasn't going to repeat this to him again. Not like this. "I came to you. I was compelled by the challenge. I hate that I sucked you in, but I've never blamed you."

"Don't hate the time we spent working together. I made my decisions too, and one of them was to spend more time with you. You really are a brilliant, amazing individual."

"Jordan and Chloe are in." Oz's voice cut through the moment. "Did I interrupt?"

"No." Like that, Graham shut down.

Boo.

"You sure? Because if you're confessing your undying love, I can come back in about five minutes." Oz sat next to me.

He had to know that implied anything but walking away.

Graham's exhale embodied frustration. "I don't understand this. You've got this one-of-a-kind woman, and you're joking about her with another guy?"

"You don't know me very well, so let me explain a couple of things," Oz said. "I'm the foil in any group. No one has ever said *Oh that Cole, he's such a joker.*"

Graham scowled and stood. "I need my laptop to start a calendar. You have dates for those appointments?"

Wait. Hear him out. Me. I swallowed the request. If Graham was closing the conversation off now, I wasn't in the mood for the rejection that would come with forcing him to listen when he wasn't open to hearing.

We fell into work. Scheduling. Planning. Never exchanging more than a few words at a time.

So much for the cards helping us work toward less tension. I wasn't doing days more of this. Did I want to put up with this for the next few weeks, or was I better off telling Graham that we could correspond via email and chat after today?

The thought of pushing him away, even if it wasn't far, made my insides curdle.

"Why teaching?" Oz's question came out of nowhere.

Graham stared blankly at Oz, seconds ticking away. He finally said, "Why did you ask?" His question held a suspicious edge.

"Luna's cards said you wanted success and fortune."

"I never used the word *fortune*." In fact, I'd specifically been careful with my phrasing because success meant different things to different people.

Oz shrugged. "Ten of Coins. Coins mean money."

"You're not possibly that simple." Graham had forgotten his work

"Pretend I am. You don't fall under that umbrella of *those who can't, teach.* You know your shit. What made you say *Fuck being paid what I'm worth. I'll teach.*"

Graham was back to the blank staring with no words.

That was super awkward. Like, chibi Luna sweat-dropping, waiting to see what came next.

"What?" Oz asked.

"I'm waiting for the follow up comment about corrupting students." Graham's voice was flat.

"I obviously don't have room to talk. I'm obsessed with the same woman, for probably very similar reasons."

Obsessed? Oz was obsessed with me? The power in the word rattled my thoughts. Was it wrong that I liked it?

fighting for it

"Success has a lot of shapes," Graham said. "For me, it includes helping other people achieve their potential."

And there was that sexy teacher vibe I adored in both men. Another thing they had in common besides me.

"Hmm." Oz grunted.

Graham scowled. "What is that? *Hmm*?"

"I respect that," Oz said.

Simple enough. They'd reached common ground without getting too snippy. Was it too soon to hope this was a trend? If so, I needed the animosity to lessen a lot faster.

Graham half closed the lid on his laptop. "What about you? You were one of the original crew, and most of them are still big names in some way. You vanished."

"I didn't choose the video game life. The video game life chose me."

I let a tiny laugh out at Oz's reply.

"Really?" Graham's flat question said he wasn't as amused.

Oz hadn't looked at a computer since we sat down. He was stretched out on the blanket, completely casual. "Cord recruited me. I fucked around there for a while, and like you, I wanted to be doing something that had more impact. I'd go into detail, but you've already checked up on me."

Graham shrugged. "I won't apologize for that."

"You sure?" Oz straightened and leaned in. "I can't needle you into feeling guilty? Because I'm getting the impression self-flagellation is your kink."

"Excuse me?"

"Do you get off on the degradation, or is it an act?"

Oz's question probably sounded strictly confrontational to anyone, especially Graham, but after last night, it held a deeper meaning for me.

The deep creases in Graham's forehead implied he wasn't impressed. "What kind of question is that? Do I beat off while I tell my reflection how shitty I am for the mistakes I've made? No."

"Would you do it while you watched someone else fuck the woman you adore? Would you suck his cock clean after he'd been inside her?"

Geez, this was making me squirm. I didn't want Oz to be so bluntly aggressive, but I also wanted to hear Graham's answer.

Red crept up Graham's neck to color his cheeks, and he clenched his jaw. "Are the rumors true, about the early days of Cord?" His question was calm, as though he were asking about the weather.

"There's a truth to most rumors. The degree of truth is the real question," Oz said.

fighting for it

Graham focused on me. "The rumors that a lot of your free time—that entire original team—was spent in one giant fuckfest of an orgy."

I was grateful Oz had already told me this, or I would have choked on the air. Hearing Graham ask about it, not knowing how he felt, made it difficult for me to hold onto my composure, regardless.

"Yup." Oz *popped* on the *p*. "That's pretty solidly true."

Graham looked between us, his gaze landing on me again. "You're being quiet. What are you thinking?"

You first. I was looking longingly at the fantasy of having both men at the same time. Not a lot of people had patience, but I did. I'd waited for three years to see Graham again, though. And before that, several years just wondering if he noticed me. And now he was right here, skirting the edges of a conversation about sex.

Could I risk a replay of the other night? Did I want to deal with his rejection again? Believing Oz would be here regardless didn't help. They were two separate entities.

I had to know. "What if it was without all the stuff Oz just said. Without the humiliation." I liked that bit, but if it wasn't for Graham, I liked other things too.

"*It*?" Graham repeated. "Watching the two of you have sex?"

When he put it that way… "No. All three of us. Or him watching us." I had to force myself not to sound timid, amid the screaming in the back of my mind that said he was going to reject me again. Worse, if he was judgmental about it, I'd have to be mad at him again.

Graham lifted the screen on his laptop, lowered his head, and drummed his fingers on the keys, not really typing.

"Luna asked you a question," Oz said.

Graham looked around—everywhere but at us. "Are the cameras on a separate network than the one I'm attached to? Uploading to the cloud? This has to be a joke."

"You knocked on her door this morning." Oz was calm. "I already mentioned how I feel about that kind of joke, and how little do you know about Luna to think she'd pull a prank like that? What purpose would it serve besides cruelty?"

I hadn't followed the thought that far, but the notion soured my soul.

"That's not it." Graham sighed, and focused on me again. "You're okay with this."

"Yes." I'd given Oz more details, but that was as much dirty talk as anything, and I wasn't that comfortable with Graham. I'd like to be… "I like the idea of sex with both of you at the same time."

"I—" Graham worked his jaw. He shut his laptop completely, rolled onto his knees, and crawled toward me on the blanket.

When he brushed his lips over mine, my heart skipped with a bittersweet blend of hope and doubt. I leaned into his mouth.

He slid his hand to the back of my neck and deepened the kiss.

My heart hammered against my ribs, threatening to break free, and I whimpered.

As if spurred by the sound, Graham nipped along my lips, before licking away the sting and sliding his tongue into my mouth.

Fuck me, this was real.

Chapter Twelve

Graham trailed his fingers through my hair and his mouth down my neck. This was tenderness blended with desire, like the perfect left of sweet meets tart cherry.

Not a single daydream I'd ever had about Graham came close to this. I needed to be a part of him. I nudged us both, my hands on his shoulders, my fists clenching his shirt, until he was sitting enough for me to climb into his lap and straddle his legs.

I was intently aware that Oz watched all of this, and that heightened my desire. He wanted to watch as much as I wanted his eyes on us, though I had no doubt he'd be happy to switch places with Graham as well.

Each kiss and touch from Graham, along my jaw, down my neck, around the curve of my ear, was delicate, as if he wanted to savor every moment.

"Are you sure this is what you want?" Graham murmured against the hollow of my neck, below my ear.

My chuckle was strained with frustration. "I'm sure, and I'm going to be offended if you ask again."

"I won't." He pressed his lips to the tender skin and traveled lower to drag his tongue along the exposed part of my chest. "I've always wondered what your freckles taste like."

"Always is a long time." A warmth brighter than the morning sun spread inside.

His light laugh hummed through my skin. "How about *far longer than I should have.*"

"What's the verdict?"

"Better than I ever imagined." Each time he shifted to kiss a new part of me, his erection pressed into me, hindered by the layers of our clothing.

The way he slid his palms up my thighs, pushing my skirt out of the way, was a stark contrast to Oz last night. Graham teased his thumbs under my panties, along my hips and waist. He moved his mouth back to my neck, sucking lightly at first, and then harder as I tilted my head to give him easier access.

I could make out with Graham all day. A different day. One where I hadn't waited years to find out what this would be like with him, and where we didn't have a captivated audience.

"I've fantasized about you for so long." It was easier to let the confession out than I thought. Oz's encouragement last night helped my courage, though

I wouldn't tell Graham quite the same things about my desires. I wanted something different from him… and to not scare him off. "About you taking me on your desk, with people passing by outside. With that thrill of getting caught."

He glided his hands closer to the center of my need, brushing the edges of my pussy. "That would have been bad."

"In real life. But in my head, it's an amazing fantasy. Especially if someone wanted to watch. To get off to the sight of you fucking me." Like Oz was now. I could hear his heavy breathing mingling with ours.

"I've had a few of those daydreams myself," Graham admitted.

Hearing that added another spark to the already roaring inferno inside, licking at my skin. Wanting to be unleashed so it could consume us both. "Fuck me while Cole watches?" I let the pleading slide into my voice.

Graham let out a strained laugh. "You have so many hidden layers." He promoted me to slide onto the blanket, then onto my back. "Let's peel away another one." He dragged my panties down my legs and tossed them aside, before kissing back up the inside of my thighs.

I squirmed at the light nibbles and scruff of his short beard on my skin. He didn't tease, as he reached my core, dragging his tongue along my slit. My groan mingled with two others and I arched into his touch.

He licked along my slick flesh, burying himself inside me, drawing up to my clit the back down again, like I was the most delicious ice cream. I moved to tangle my fingers in his hair, to draw him in closer, and Oz grabbed my wrists, pinning them above my head.

Oh geez. With Graham between my legs, licking, sucking, and tongue fucking me, and Oz keeping me from doing more than squirming, I was a bundle of nerve endings. Pleasure surged inside, inching toward climax.

Graham pressed his fingers to my clit as he probed my opening. I strained against Oz's grip, and he tightened his hold, fingers digging into my wrists in the most delicious way.

Orgasm spilled through me. My cries of ecstasy and pumping hips spurred Graham to lick and finger harder, devouring me until it was too much. Until my body shuddered.

Oz let go of my wrists and pressed tender kisses to each of my bare shoulders. "Fuck, you're gorgeous when you come," he whispered.

I flushed.

Graham pulled away, and I heard the tear of foil. He knelt between my legs, nudged my opening with the head of his cock, and slid inside me.

This wasn't a hard thrust, it was a slow, delicious stretch as I opened up to accept his length, stretching out with each inch, until he was buried to the hilt.

Graham withdrew to the tip, before plunging into me again, over and over, in an agonizingly delicious build to a steady pace.

Was I greedy for wanting more? I had two men watching and helping me writhe in pleasure. I was going to take advantage of it. I rolled my head back to meet Oz's gaze. "I want to taste you."

That yummy, animalistic smile was back. He moved to kneel at the side of head, his cock in his hand.

Graham gripped my hips, pumping faster, when Oz pressed against my lips.

I opened hungrily, letting Oz in, swirling my tongue around his shaft as best I could, while Graham built to a frantic pace, slamming inside me.

I pushed down the top of my dress enough to expose my breasts, and kneaded, pinching my nipples, tugging for that extra spark of sensation.

Oz worked his hand faster along his cock, his grunts growing louder as his rhythm grew faster.

fighting for it

Graham moved his thumb to my clit, teasing the still tender flesh, coaxing while he fucked me hard and fast.

I didn't know where to focus. What sensation I wanted more of beyond *all of it*. I tumbled into overload.

A salty spurt hit the back of my throat when Oz came, but he didn't stay in my mouth. Cum slid down my jaw, another burst hitting my chest. My breasts.

I clenched the blanket in my fists as another orgasm stole my breath and my thoughts. Nothing existed around us, and at the same time I felt everything. Tasted it. Heard limitless desire in a duet of male groans.

Graham squeezed my hip tighter, his jerky movements stuttering to a stall, before he finished in a slow, winding down crescendo of movement and sound.

As everything stopped, I slowly became aware of the sunshine on my skin. The rustle of the wind in the trees. Grass poking through the blanket and tickling my back. Graham's mouth on mine as he shared Oz's taste with me, kissing hungrily.

"God, you're amazing." Graham was breathless.

"Takes one to know one."

He laughed into the kiss and pulled away.

Oz brushed a loose strand of hair from my forehead. From this angle, he looked angelic. "Don't move," he said. "Either of you."

Not like I could if I wanted to.

Oz returned a moment later with two washcloths, tossed one at Graham, and took his time wiping me clean. A girl could get used to this kind of tender treatment. Ah, who was I kidding? I was already hooked.

We collapsed in a pile, my head on Graham's shoulder and Oz pressed into my back, arm around my waist.

The best thing about chocolate sandwich cookie ice cream was finding a whole cookie hidden away in the creamy sweetness. The most dangerous thing about chocolate sandwich cookie ice cream was finding one whole cookie, and following it to another, and another, until the entire pint was gone.

As I lay on a blanket on the grass, wrapped in sunshine and sandwiched between Oz and Graham, I knew I was in the same kind of I'm-about-to-eat-the-whole-pint trouble. I was willing to just keep snacking on this sandwich cookie of us, over and over, until I was overstuffed.

Chibi-Luna giggled at my unintentional innuendo. Sometimes I cracked me up.

Oz trailed his fingers through my hair, as I listened to his heartbeat.

fighting for it

Graham lay behind me, hand on my hip and thumb tracing a short path back and forth along my skin. "You didn't look bothered by anything Cole said." Graham's tone was thoughtful. "The humiliation. The self-flagellation."

If I told him what I was thinking, he could call me a freak. Say this was all a big mistake and walk away. With the sun beating down on us, and a soft breeze brushing my skin, the concern didn't hold any weight. "I thought it was hot."

"You did." Graham sounded surprised, but in a good way. "The idea of that turns you on?"

"Being used as a set of holes, and punished and told how dirty I am for the entire thing, while I choke on a thick cock and get covered in sticky bodily fluids? Yes." The next bit was the important part. Maybe I should've led with it. "In the heat of the moment, with someone I trust, as long as I know it's part of the sex and not real. And there's a lot of reassurance after."

Oz leaned up enough to brush his lips over the top of my head. "Doesn't she say the most brilliant things?"

"Hmm."

Wasn't that Oz's thing? I didn't like the idea of them both relying on the vague grunt.

"What is that? That *hmm*?" Oz asked.

Apparently he didn't care for it being used against him, either.

"It means I don't have an answer."

Graham was still here, so his hesitation couldn't be all bad, but I wanted that reassurance.

Chapter Thirteen

The three of us spent the rest of the day working and enjoying each other's company. Apparently all it took for Oz and Graham to get along were a pair of good orgasms.

Not that I blamed them. The experience left me wrapped in a pleasant ball of warmth. Graham's non-answers weighed on me, but his actions after made doubt easier to ignore.

It was almost nine at night when Graham stood reluctantly. "I should be on my way."

It wasn't late, late, but given he showed up at my place twelve hours ago, it had been a long day of work.

The break in the middle was pretty incredible though.

"You're welcome to stay," Oz said. "I've got room."

He had a way bigger bed than mine, that was for sure. Did I know because I'd had to sneak a peek at his bedroom more than once? Duh.

Graham shouldered his laptop bag. "Thanks, but no. This was a lot of fun, but I'm not going to make a habit of it."

Of... what? The statement didn't make any sense.

After Graham left, Oz tugged me into his lap and dragged his nose along the back of my neck. "I don't understand how anyone could resist making a habit of you."

Graham hadn't been talking about me. Had he? "I think he mean the three-person sex." That was a more reasonable alternative from the outside, but still not one I liked. "You're okay with what happened today, aren't you?"

"I told you I was." Oz's reply was kind.

"That was before it happened."

He wrapped his arms around my waist, and grasped my fingers. "I still have my doubts about Graham when it comes to me calling him more than an acquaintance. But if you like him, and he's not hurting you, yeah, I'm fine with it. And if you want me there for some of it, even better. Turns out I like watching you fuck. No surprise there, since I like watching you do a lot of things."

As we made our way to bed that night, Oz was wonderfully understanding that I wanted to skip the sex and just fall asleep with him wrapped around me.

fighting for it

I wanted to spend Sunday with Oz too, but we both had prior plans. Still, waking up to his kisses and someone else making me coffee was a luxury I could get addicted to.

He was driving me back to my place when his phone rang. He glanced at the screen for half a second. "It's Jake."

"I don't mind if you answer," I said.

Oz did exactly that. "Hey, Jake."

"Cole. How's it going? I need a minute."

"Sure."

I'd met Jake before. He placed Oz's people in new positions when their apprenticeships ended. I tried to busy myself by watching the mountain scenery. It was rude to eavesdrop, but it wasn't like I could go in the other room, and with the call on speaker…

"That woman you were introducing on Friday night. You saw the news about her?" Jake asked.

Me. I was *that woman*. I wouldn't assume this was bad news, except there wasn't any other kind about me out there right now.

Oz's jaw was set hard. "I did. I also know *the news* is tabloid hype."

"Funny how a piece of a—"

"If you wouldn't say it to her face, don't say it to me." Oz bit off the words. "I'd hate to have to kill a business relationship because you're a misinformed asshole."

Jake's chuckle was tight. "That's actually why I'm calling. I can't place your people anymore. I won't work with someone who supports the kind of loose ethics that young woman has."

Oh geez. I sank lower in my seat.

"You're wrong." There was no hesitation in Oz's retort. "About Luna. About the entire situation. But I'm glad you didn't hide it. You're right, we won't work together again." He disconnected, cutting Jake off.

I wanted to curl up in a ball and hide.

"This is on him, not you." Oz settled his hand on my knee.

The touch was comforting, but not enough to erase the situation. "You just lost a business contact because of me."

"No. He's gone because of himself, not you. You understand that."

"I guess." Not really. I heard the sincerity and command in Oz's words, but if this was Day Two of Luna is an Evil Mastermind, it didn't feel like it was going to fade into the background.

Oz squeezed my leg gently. "I'm here because I want to be. Because you're worth it. Not because we're fucking. Because you deserve more."

fighting for it

No one *deserved* just for existing. Not beyond the essentials. I didn't know how to argue that, though. "I guess."

Chapter Fourteen

The next few days were a slog of scheduling times I could meet with my friends' famous friends, and scouring ads for jobs and apartments.

Violet got me airtime with Sadie and Grayson, which went so well. They were friendly, made me feel at ease, and was about as perfect an introduction to this process as I could've hoped for.

Wednesday, Graham was taking me to meet his sister. This wasn't like a *let me introduce you to the family* thing. Though, there was a distinctly loud part of me insisting that in a way, it was.

Adrienne was an artist, and she was going to draw me, just a cartoon version, to use as part of my branding.

Who was I that I needed branding?

I was supposed to be myself. Which for me meant overthinking ten different outfits in a span of two minutes, until half my wardrobe, from cutoffs and a T-shirt to my nicest interview outfit, blanketed my bed.

I tugged a corset out of the back of the closet. Violet got this for me a few years back, for

Halloween. It was pale blue and white, with gauzy, wire-framed wings. It was absolutely not the kind of thing that someone wore for the day-to-day. As I laced it on, and twisted this way and that in front of the mirror, it made me feel absolutely magical.

And now that I had that happy glow, I could put on something more practical. I was reaching for a T-shirt in the discarded pile that said *Gamer Girls Do It Better*, when someone knocked.

I opened the door to Graham.

"I'm early, I know. I…" His gaze fell on me and he trailed off. "Wow." He drew the knuckle of his index finger lightly up my bare shoulder, dropping his touch short of my neck. "It's always been hard to keep my hands to myself around you, but I don't know if it's possible anymore."

"Why would you have to?" I could be coy, but he was so freaking close and if I was going to spend more time with him, I needed some clarity. "I get it. Before, you were my teacher. Now, you're not."

"I don't know what you expect me to say, Luna."

There were a handful of things I wanted to hear, but there was one specifically that needed to happen sooner rather than later. "Stop with the mixed signals. You push me away for my own good. You want more. Oz is in the way. You don't want to keep your hands to yourself… There's no possible way you don't know I'm interested."

Graham reached for me, and I pressed my palm to his to stop him.

"If you do this, no more *but we shouldn't* after." I didn't know where the directness came from.

He gave a half smile and chuckle, twisted his wrist to break the contact between us, and rested his hand on my cheek. "That's fair."

He brushed his lips over mine and my heart skipped. When he pressed into me, pushing me back into the apartment, my body molded and yielded to his.

There was no tentative exploration like there had been the other day at Oz's. Graham didn't stop pushing until my back was to the wall. He dragged his mouth along my jaw and up to nibble my earlobe. "I'm not going to do any of that stuff you and he talked about."

I noticed he didn't say Oz's name. "You don't have to. My fantasies about you are different."

"There's more than just *on the desk at school*?" Graham moved his mouth down to my collarbone, teasing his thumbs along the top of my breasts, above the hem of the corset.

Doubt whispered in. "I'm not the only one who's been… You've had…" Maybe I didn't want to know if he wasn't fantasizing about me.

"I can't count the number of times I've beat myself raw, to images of taking you, well, anywhere you wanted." He dragged a finger lightly over my nipple, drawing a tingle even though layers of fabric.

I sighed happily at the touch. "I love it when we're thinking the same things."

"Fuck, I wish we had more time right now."

"You were fifteen minutes early," I reminded him.

The sound that rumbled up from deep in his chest filled me with need. "Fifteen minutes isn't nearly enough time for what I want to do to you. I'll have to leave us wanting."

I'd been wanting for a decade. I also hated being late or keeping anyone waiting. I jutted out my lower lip.

He kissed the pout away. "What's wrong?"

"I hate that we can't just let passion take over and ignore the rest of the world."

"Me too. But we have enough time for something." He teased his fingers under the waistband of my jeans.

I let out a light laugh at the combination of ticklish and seductive touch. "What did you have in mind?"

Graham flipped the button on my jeans and dragged down the zipper. "I realized the other day that I have a new favorite sight." He slipped his hand lower, under my trousers and over my panties. "Watching you come."

"I bet I look silly." How else was I supposed to respond to that?

He brushed his lips over mine. "You look stunning. Always." He slipped the crotch of my underwear aside, and drew his fingers lightly along my bare skin.

I parted my lips in a long moan and he leaned into swallow the noise, as he parted my folds.

The longer he kissed me and teased along my pussy, the slicker I grew. He slipped his fingers near my opening, and away again.

I rocked against his touch, desire building inside. The door was still open, and the noise of traffic drifted in, along with the distant chatter of people on the sidewalk. No one was going to come back here, but the possibility they might cranked my anticipation a notch higher.

Graham moved to my clit to circle the swollen nub. Wowza, he had skilled fingers. My breath came in short pants the longer he stroked me.

Orgasm crashed in, washing over and through me. Was I gasping? Screaming? I didn't know or care.

As my world slowly swam back into focus as Graham eased off, but my legs didn't recover so quickly. As I caught my breath, his pressing me to the wall held me upright.

My gaze landed on my digital clock, and reality whispered back in. We'd gone from early to late. "I don't have time to change."

"Never change. I like you just the way you are."

"You're a goof." I wasn't complaining. About any of this. His weight pressing into me, his erection digging into my leg, and the light mood in the room. In fact the only complaint I had was that we couldn't stay and play. "I meant my top."

"I want to keep the jokes going by saying something about him not being here. Is that appropriate? Am I allowed to joke about Cole?" Hearing that name pass Graham's lips made things even better. It was another barrier knocked aside.

"Depends on the joke, but you don't have to pretend he doesn't exist. This doesn't change what he and I have." More reality. "You realize that don't you?"

"I do. I'm still processing, but the fact that I get you—this—makes it easier. Don't change the top. You look magical, and Adrienne will work magic from the visual."

Heat flushed me at his use of *magical* and that it mirrored my thoughts.

Given neither of us liked to be late, with a little extra effort and reluctance, we peeled apart, and were on our way.

Apparently I'd already gotten addicted to Oz's frequent touch, because I was disappointed that Graham kept his hands to himself as we drove. Now that the initial making out was over, would this be awkward?

I didn't want that. I wanted to be the person I was when Oz asked me about my fantasies. When Graham was being wishy washy. This wasn't normal, was it? For me to slide into *okay, I'm seeing both of you now*, with so little hesitation.

Then again, when had I ever been normal? "How long have you known where I was?" I asked.

"I knew you stayed in state. Beyond that? Not until the other day. Following you would've made it harder to ignore you. Also, it's creepy."

Right. In movies it was romance. In real life it was stalking. "You just waited until a single night to learn everything about what I'd been up to."

"The things I want to know about you, I won't find online. I won't learn any other way than spending time with you."

Okay, that was super sweet. Like, chibi Luna swooning and melting kind of sweet.

"I did look up a lot about Cole, though," Graham said.

fighting for it

"Should I be jealous?" I teased.

Graham shook his head. "I think that's my line."

"I hope you won't be. Jealous, that is. I don't expect you to turn it off *now*, like flipping a switch, but if you could get there…"

He brushed his hand over mine, pausing to squeeze before moving back to the steering wheel. "How've you been? Genuinely. Not this fake bullshit most people expect."

"Good. I've been genuinely good. Finding work is tough, which means things like making rent are tough, but I have more than the necessities, and people looking out for me. You? You said private tutoring."

"I'm happy I get to keep teaching," Graham said. "And I noticed you've kept up with tech. Despite… restrictions." He wasn't asking.

I'd all but confirmed that already. "What you're implying would've violated my probation. Are you wearing a wire?"

"You had your hands all over me earlier. You tell me." He navigated the streets with ease, taking us closer to the mountains and the edge of the valley.

"Well… there was something in your pants," I said playfully. "But it was pretty big for a modern listening device."

"Hard drives took up more space when I was made."

I couldn't help but snicker at his phrasing. "*Made*? Humans call that being born."

"I— Uh— What are you implying?" His defensive stutter was exaggerated.

I thought my implication was obvious. "Are you a Cylon?"

"N— n— *no*."

I wasn't convinced, and I was struggling to hold my laughter back enough so I could speak. This was easy. Fun. Exactly what I missed about Graham. "If you are, you should know I won't betray the entire planet, no matter how good the sex is."

"So much for that mission." He sighed heavily.

"Wait. Don't let that stop you from trying. You can't give up that easily."

"I'm definitely not giving up. You already have the codes to bring down my defense system." His voice shifted to serious.

A knot formed in my chest at the abrupt shift in tone. "That was cheesy."

"At least I don't tell dad jokes. And you have to admit, it was sweet."

The best kind of sweet. "Better than chocolate…" I trailed off when he turned onto one of the roads leading to University parking.

"Are you okay?" Graham asked.

fighting for it

"This place has a lot of memories." I hadn't been back since graduation. Most of my college time was amazing, but those few mistakes—like the one I made with Tiff—were enough to spoil a lot of the rest.

Graham squeezed my hand. "I didn't even think to warn you, I'm sorry. Adrienne spends a lot of time up here in the art building, because she has teacher friends who let her use a studio. That's where we're meeting her."

"It's okay. I'll be okay." I had to get over it eventually. Didn't I?

Chapter Fifteen

We made our way to the Art building, and Graham led me to one of the rooms near the rear entrance. There was a woman near the front of the room, head down, attention focused on a drawing pad. I saw the resemblance to Graham instantly.

"Pst," Graham whispered.

She looked up and smiled when she saw us. "Hey." She gestured for us to join her, and gave Graham a hug when he was close enough. "Luna?"

"Hi." I liked her warmth.

"I'm Adrienne. So glad to meet you. I love your corset. Those wings are everything."

Yup. I liked her a lot. I spun so she could see my back. "Isn't the whole thing amazing?"

"I was going to say magical."

"That's what I told her," Graham said.

Adrienne tugged gently at one wing. "Magical Fae Luna. That's it." She returned to her chair and started sketching.

That all happened quickly. Not that I minded. No reason to stress about if she'd like me. If I'd like her.

fighting for it

Her pencil scratched across paper and she stuck her tongue out just a smidge while she sketched. "So you're the girl who got my big brother arrested."

My stomach plummeted into my shoes.

Graham coughed.

Adrienne looked up, eyes wide. "Oh my god, I'm so sorry. That came out wrong. I didn't mean—"

"How is she going to take that in a good way?" Graham's question was sharp.

"I was teasing, I promise." Apology rang in Adrienne's voice. "I didn't mean to strike any nerves. Graham's told me so much about you."

He had?

"And I have nothing but the deepest respect for you," Adrienne said. "You've done amazing things, and you're so brilliant. I'm honored to get to sketch you." She sounded sincere. She held up a line art, chibi version of me, complete with the wings on the corset.

The art, even though it was rough, was fantastic, and I'd said dumb things to new people plenty of times. I understood. "I can't believe you just drew that. I love it. Do you do this professionally?"

She blushed and returned to the drawing, this time with colored pencils. "I do 3D rendering for a commercial architect. But I'd love to work in games. Is that silly?"

"Not silly at all. Me too." Okay, now I liked her again.

"And I really am sorry," Adrienne said. "I don't blame you for what happened. Not even a teensy, tiny, minuscule bit. I know Graham blames himself. He's like that. White knight always coming to someone's rescue. He's been sticking up for me for as long as I can remember." She was a rambler too. Full respect for that.

I also liked hearing these snippets about Graham from someone else. "That's really sweet."

"It's especially useful when he comes to my defense at family dinners, when Mom and Dad are asking me when I'm going to meet a nice man, settle down, and give them grandkids."

I may not be ready for this conversation.

Graham chuckled nervously. "I have to take the heat off you, so I don't get it either."

"But now that he's got you, you've got at least five or ten more baby-making years than I do."

"*Adrienne*," Graham all but shouted.

I laughed.

"Oh, God, I did it again." Adrienne looked horrified. "It was a joke. I promise. I'm not usually this bad."

Graham sighed. "She's frequently this bad."

fighting for it

"Okay, so I am. I'm horrible at reading the room. Especially when I'm nervous. Always sticking my foot in my mouth. I didn't mean what I said; I just have a weird sense of humor."

"It's okay. I promise." And it was. There were few things I understood better than people thinking I was weird because I said things they didn't expect.

We chatted a little more while Adrienne added colors to the picture. I loved it even more now. It was me in my corset, wielding a deck of tarot cards.

She promised to digitize it and email it to me within the next couple of days. The three of us said our *goodbyes* and Graham and I left her to get back to her own art.

On the way out, I wanted to wander through the Computer Science building. Actually, I didn't, but I figured as long as we were here it was a good time to push past more of my discomfort. The school itself had nothing to do with what happened, other than being where I met Tiff. I'd learned a lot of wonderful things here as well as meeting Graham. I wanted to bring more of those moments to the front of my mind.

A voice filtered out from one of the rooms as well strolled down the hall. The sign out front said

Professor Erol

Ethics in Programming, Development, and Computer Science

Open to the Public

I grabbed Graham's arm and tugged him toward the door. "We have a little more time, don't we?"

"This isn't the kind of lecture you want to hear."

I twisted my mouth and stared at him, waiting for him to take it back. "I think it is. This kind of stuff fascinates me."

"The topic, yes. The speaker? No. This isn't a *let's learn* kind of thing. I guarantee it's going to be a self-important man ranting about who should and shouldn't be allowed in computing. I worked with him, and I've never heard him do anything but."

I tugged Graham in the back entrance and into seats near the top of the amphitheater. "He's not going to just rant. I can sift through the opinions to hear worthwhile," I said. Ethics were subjective anyway, and this was free knowledge.

The lecture was only about ten minutes in, and Prof. Erol was wrapping up his introduction.

And then, as he launched into a diatribe about how teaching certain types of coding in school only led to malfeasance, my stomach dropped. I was watching a real life Professor Umbridge condescend to a room full of captive ears about the evils of the magic that was security programming.

When he used my name as an example, calling me a vile specimen of immorality, Graham actually freaking growled.

fighting for it

Graham half-rose in his seat and I yanked him back down.

"You were right." My voice was tight. "Let's just go." I wanted to be anywhere else. Now.

Graham clenched his jaw.

"Please," I begged.

Graham nodded, and we headed toward the exit.

"Does the truth bother you?" Erol's voice hit our backs.

Graham huffed, his nostrils flared, and turned to the stage. "The truth? No. The prejudiced meanderings of a misogynist? Quite a bit." He squeezed my hand.

While I loved seeing him standing tall, his voice booming across the amphitheater like the professor I'd fallen for, this wasn't the situation I wanted to see it in.

"Since we're speaking about you, would you like to provide a defense?" Erol asked. "Ladies and gentlemen, the sole reason the school updated our ethics policy a few years back. If you'll note the young lady on his arm, you can see he hasn't learned his lesson."

I wanted to curl up in a little ball and hide, but I stood there, expression blank, refusing to let this man beat me down verbally.

"I do have thoughts on the subject, yes." Graham's tone was firm. Confident. "If we start placing limits on innovation, we stop innovating. People need to be allowed to explore all possible avenues when they embark on discovery, and if we limit the scope of education, students will find the information somewhere else. Frequently without the structure and knowledge of an experienced individual to guide them."

Geez that was sexy. I was having flashbacks to that very first class I took from him, and why I'd been infatuated before we ever spoke one-on-one.

"Obviously, we need to use considerations and reason in each decision, but we need to provide the tools for others to do the same," Graham said. "Will someone use that knowledge for things we don't agree with? Always. That can't be stopped. But the negative can be minimized if we're guiding people rather than pointing them toward a shiny red button and telling them *do not touch*."

Erol's laugh was more like a barking pig. "Thank you for proving my point, Mr. Anderson. Give an otherwise intelligent man a bit of snatch and he's willing to abandon all reason. Which brings me to my next point—the proliferation of pornography on the Internet."

"That's not a valid counter." Graham's voice carried, but Erol continued to talk over him.

fighting for it

"Now that's a man who's never had good sex," a woman nearby said, just loudly enough for us and those around us to hear.

A few snickers rolled through the back of the hall.

I followed the comment to find Judith standing.

"You have something to add, young lady?" Erol was focused on us again, as Judith joined us.

"Ma'am, or Ms. Walsh will do fine, thank you." Judith's voice carried as well as either man's, and her presence commanded attention.

Chibi Luna was back in my head, swooning. *So scary. So amazing.*

"I see, Miss Walsh. Enlighten us." Erol sneered.

The corner of Judith's mouth tugged up. "*Ms.* But I understand your reluctance to accept peers who don't have a dick."

Between Judith and Graham, they expanded on what Graham opened with, crafting a compelling statement about growing knowledge rather than limiting it, and how prohibition is never the answer, even in schooling.

A pair of men in security uniforms approached us. "You need to leave campus." One reached for Judith.

She stepped away, eyebrows raised. "If I were to let you touch me, you wouldn't know what to do with me."

"We're leaving. That was all we wanted in the first place." I headed toward the door and prayed Graham would follow.

He fell into step behind me.

Judith joined us, on my other side. "Looks like we get an escort to the parking lot." She jerked her head behind us.

A glance confirmed security was following us.

This wasn't as humiliating as when I was arrested a few years ago, but it certainly summoned and attached itself to those memories. And once again Graham was involved, further sinking his reputation and career.

"You look good." Judith's compliment drew me back to the now. "Even in there, you looked good."

I gave her a weak smile. "Thanks."

"I don't believe we've met. I'm Graham Anderson." He extended his hand.

"Pleasure to meet you." She reached across me for the handshake. "Nice to see that like everything else he said in there, the parts about you were untrue."

Graham tangled his fingers with mine. "You know that from three minutes of stilted debate?"

"It's a lot more complicated than that, but that helps." Judith looked past him, to me. "How are you holding up?"

fighting for it

"Aside from not being able to find a job, and the fact that the world runs on money, I'm great." I meant to say that bit in my head. Oopsie.

Her eyes grew wide. "You can't… Absolutely ridiculous."

"It's okay." I didn't mean to dump on her. Not only a stranger but a boyfriend's ex-wife—that wasn't convoluted at all. "Graham and Cole are helping me rebuild my reputation. I'll come out of things fine." And I would.

"So this is your Lancelot. The knight who thinks he's done you wrong and needs to make right for his queen." Judith's tone was one of respect. "I bet Cole loves you, Graham." Her voice twisted a notch.

"I hear your sarcasm, and I assure you he does not," Graham said.

"Regardless. Luna, give me your number. I see interesting opportunities all the time, and I'd be happy to drop your name."

I smiled. "All right. Thank you." The brief exchange made me feel a whole lot better.

As long as I could push aside the unpleasantness from the amphitheater, and the quiet whisper asking how much worse it would get before it got better.

Chapter Sixteen

I spent the next three days in one podcast and interview after another. At least it felt like it.

Between Hunter and Oz, they'd gotten me on to seven different shows. Since most were pre-recorded, I spent at least two hours in each studio. Add the bus rides to that, and I barely had time to sleep, with no time to see Oz, Graham, or Violet. At least I got to text them, and I was the goofy dork who scrolled through those messages over and over when I needed a mood boost.

I understood that the interviews were fluff pieces, meant to show the fun side of me, but that also meant I was repeating a lot of the same, with no real substance. I crashed every night when I got home, and dragged myself out of bed to extra coffee every morning.

This would be worth it though. The payoff. The success. Getting a job.

Even though the *thanks but no thanks* letters were stacking up.

I was grateful for Sunday morning. I'd see Oz and Graham today. Sure, it was to do more work—

compare notes, regroup, and change any plans that required it—but I was still seeing my guys.

My guys. The term rolled easily through my thoughts and warmed me from the inside out. I'd rather spend the day cuddling, but seeing them would help.

I grabbed a vibrant plum sundress from my closet, and tossed a light sweater with embroidered flowers over it. The colors were another accent to brighten my mood.

The instant I opened the door to Oz, he cupped my face between his palms and crushed his mouth to mine in a breath-stealing kiss that drew out my exhaustion and replaced it with comfort and adoration. He finally pulled away to press his lips to the top of my head.

"I missed you." His words sank into my skull and my soul.

The world was instantly a better place. "Same."

"Shall we?" He offered his elbow.

I grabbed my purse and laptop, locked the door, and hooked my hand around his arm.

When we reached the truck Graham was waiting on the passenger side, door open.

"Oh." That made me smile even wider. "I thought you were meeting us up there. Not that I mind."

He grasped my fingertips and kissed the back of my knuckles. "Change of plans. I wanted to see you now."

"Yay." I'd clap, except I didn't want to let go of him. "Three way date." I liked this Graham more than ever. Direct. Sweet. With me.

It was a snug fit with the three of us in the truck, but not uncomfortable. In fact, sandwiched between my guys was about the best thing ever.

My apartment was only a few minutes from the freeway, then Oz was taking us into the mountains, toward his place.

"Okay, so wait." I put more pieces together about Graham being here. Was he becoming okay with this entire arrangement? "Does that mean we're all friends now?"

"I'm hoping you and I are more than friends at this point," Graham said.

"But yes," Oz agreed.

The weight inside was lifting, leaving feathers and sunshine and joy behind.

The truck rattled and bounced with every bump, but Oz navigated the turns and inclines with practiced ease. "How do you feel about competition gaming?"

"I wouldn't do it myself." Random, weird question. I liked it. "It's cool that it exists, and with the right players and game, it's fun to watch."

fighting for it

"Judith called me last night—"

"Do you talk to her a lot?" Graham cut him off.

Jealousy poked me, but it didn't take much to shove it aside. Oz was here with me, not with her. Besides, I liked her, regardless of how brief our conversations had been, and I didn't want a reason for that to change.

"I really don't," Oz said. "More in the last few weeks than in the last few months. But she mentioned meeting Graham, and said she had three media passes for a competition exhibition that's coming up. Said we should all be there Thursday night."

Watching gaming, with these two, and just having fun? Epic. Doing it surrounded by more crowds where I needed to be the two-dimensional version of myself? Boo. But this was all part of the plan. This was what I needed to find an in. "I'm free."

"Same." Graham slid his hand under mine, palm up, and wove his fingers through mine. "Are you all right?"

I'd let my exhaustion bleed into my voice, and hadn't meant to. "Totally fine." I summoned the internal sunshine again, to match the warmth peeking over the tops of the mountains.

"Don't do that. Don't ever think you have to hide how you feel." There was a light edge to Oz's voice.

I wasn't faking happy, I'd simply rather stay with joy than slide into unpleasant feelings. "I'm not."

Graham squeezed my hand. "If you're not up for Tuesday night, we don't have to do it."

"I'm not going to turn the opportunity down. I'm a little filtered is all. A day to recharge with my two favorite men, and I'll be fine." Unless we worked all day, setting more appointments to fill my calendar with talking to people.

I swallowed the train of thought that would lead into blahness. Oz's and Graham's company was better than cupcakes and rainbows, and when they were like this, their energy was healing.

Oz's quiet sigh tickled my insecurity. Was he disappointed in me? I didn't want that.

"You ever play the original Hoarde games?" Graham's question was an obvious and welcome right turn in the conversation. "Before Digital Media ruined them?"

Cord's flagship title when they were a brand new company.

"I played them to death." Oz snorted. Of course he did. He helped write them.

I shook my head. "Not so much. The whole FPS, shoot-to-kill isn't my thing." I didn't have a problem with the video game violence when it was as pixelated as those games had been, but I hated the tension of sneaking around, waiting for something to jump out at me.

"I played those games so much." Graham sounded nostalgic. "They got me through pre-grad."

Oz laughed. An actual chuckle. "They got me out of having to do pre-grad." He'd learned most of his skills on the job, rather than going to college.

Every time I remembered that, I was impressed. "You know what? I've been talking about myself all week, and I already know about me. You guys should talk about you." I knew surprisingly little considering how much time I'd spent with each of them. They'd done an effective job of never letting the conversations delve too deeply into their personal lives.

"On one condition," Graham said.

What was I supposed to do with a reply like that?

I chose to be amused. "Talking about yourselves requires a negotiation?"

Oz nodded. "In this case it does. Terms are, you have to take a day off."

Wasn't this Graham's deal?

"I *have* to?"

"No work at all today," Graham said.

Oh gosh golly gee darn. "But why?" I let the mock despair bleed into my voice, trying to make it obvious I was joking.

Oz headed toward an exit. We were miles from his place. "Change of plans. We're doing something different today."

"It's going to be gorgeous and sunny," Graham said.

Oz glanced at him. "Picnic?"

"You don't strike me as a *picnic* kind of guy," Graham countered.

I had the distinct impression I was being set up. And I loved it.

Oz squeezed my knee. "I'm a make-my-baby-girl-happy kind of guy."

I wrinkled my nose at the nickname.

"No?" He glanced between me and the road.

I shook my head. "You're just not great with the names. You didn't come up with yours, did you?"

His clenched jaw was all the reply I needed. Where was he taking us? Along a series of hard packed dirt roads, up a back mountain path.

"What's the story there, with the name?" I'd asked before, and he'd always brushed off the question.

"You have to agree to the deal first." Graham was taking his side. How gloriously, wonderfully silly.

"It's not even your story. *Fine.*" I couldn't help my grin as I let out an exaggerated sigh. "We'll have

fighting for it

a picnic. But only so I can learn things about you two."

We pulled around a tight curve and came to a stop at the edge of a huge clearing that was native grass and wildflowers. It wasn't really a park. It was like a tiny cove of amazing, tucked away in the mountains.

Graham grabbed a blanket out of the lockbox in the back of the truck, and Oz grabbed a cooler.

"So this was all spontaneous and you just came up with it on the drive?" I asked playfully as we laid out the blanket.

"No one ever said that." Oz pulled me to sit next to him.

"The two of you have been talking—plotting even—with each other when I'm not around." It was perfect. "And getting along enough to make plans." I fit perfectly resting against Oz, especially with Graham on my other side.

"We have." Graham reached into the cooler. He handed each of us a can of iced coffee, and extracted a bowl of fruit.

I caught a glimpse of more food, sandwiches maybe. "How long do you plan for us to spend out here?"

"As long as you want." Graham popped the top on his drink and took a sip.

Oz set his can aside, and reached for the food. "This way, there are no excuses for checking in on anything."

"It's brilliant." Better than cake or ice cream or long drawn out conversations about the most efficient bash scripts ever written in Python.

Oz set the bowl of fruit on the blanket between us, plucked a slice of strawberry out, and trailed it along my bottom lip.

I gasped at the light touch, and drew my tongue along the same path, licking away the sweet-tart juice.

He pushed the fruit into my mouth, and I drew his finger in with my tongue. His groan was more delicious than the fruit.

"Now that's not fair." Graham's protest was playful. "We've been here less than ten minutes and you two are already at it."

The corner of Oz's mouth tugged up, and he faced Graham. "No one's leaving you out."

"No?" Graham challenged.

"Nope. I'm happy to feed you fruit, too."

Uh, first, what? And second, *hot.* "Yes, please." I didn't realize I'd said the last bit out loud until Graham raised his brows.

Oz plucked a piece of melon from the bowl next, and pressed it to Graham's lips.

fighting for it

It was alluring watching Graham react the same way I had. So that was what it looked like from the outside.

And Oz's moan when Graham sucked on his fingers…

Wowza.

Pink crept up Graham's neck, and he scooted back on the blanket. "You brought bowls or something, right?"

He may be pulling away, but the tension in the air didn't dissipate.

Could I push things further? I wanted to.

I'd been promised answers, and maybe I could use that to my advantage. "The nickname—Oz—did Judith come up with it?"

"Judith is capable of a large number of things. She's not a creative individual, though. Chloe came up with the name."

Someone else I had all the respect for. Chloe was one of those original Cord staffers who was still with Rinslet today. She'd been their head writer when the company started, and was responsible for the story line on most of the X games. She was their COO now.

I met her a few days ago, doing a podcast with her partner Jordan. She wasn't just brilliant, she was also kind and totally fun.

"You've got such a fascinating past, Cole." Graham's voice was a blend of awe and envy. But not in a mean way.

"It's not really. I simply avoid talking about the boring bits."

The heat between them had cooled, and I wanted it back. Maybe I wasn't so brilliant as I thought, if I couldn't fan this existing spark.

Chapter Seventeen

"Be fair," Graham said. "You don't talk about most of the bits."

"You worked on the original team. You get to look back and say *I helped start that.*" I loved modern tech, but there was a teensy bit of me that was eternally sad that I'd never have a haven to be part of something as groundbreaking as Cord and their original games.

"Oh yeah, that too," Graham said.

I studied him, trying to puzzle out the words. "What bits were you talking about?"

Oz finished his can and crammed it into the small trash bag we had sitting next to us. "He meant the orgies."

Graham shrugged. "I led a sheltered life. My parents gave me a video to watch about sex, rather than having the talk with me themselves, and it was pretty much limited to *penis goes in vagina and babies happen.*"

"But you've expanded your horizons since." Did Oz sound... hopeful?

"I have. But when I was in my early twenties, a blow job was naughty. Group sex? That only happened in bad porn."

"To be fair, most porn was bad when we were in our early twenties."

At Oz's statement, Graham chuckled. "True. But I don't know if it's better now, or just more prolific."

This was better than Oz and Graham getting along. It was actually friendly.

"Three people aren't quite a *group*," Oz said, "but there are a lot fewer limbs to keep track of."

Inspiration struck. "Let's play a game."

"All right," Graham agreed easily.

"What are we playing?" Oz sounded more hesitant.

The kind of game that helped people open up, without feeling like twenty questions. "Firsts."

"Which is...?" Oz better not be a hard sell.

Graham leaned in, an easy smile on his face. "It's like *Truth or Dare* meets *Never Have I Ever*."

"Sounds complicated." Oz hadn't said *yes* yet, but he also hadn't said *no*. "And how do you know that?"

Probably the same way I did. "It was big on campus."

"All right," Oz's sigh was exaggerated. "How do we play *Firsts*?"

fighting for it

In my head, chibi Luna clapped and squealed in delight... and a smidge of anticipation. This game frequently ended with kissing or making out. I could get that here regardless, but this way was a different kind of fun.

"We each take a turn picking *first time you ever...* events, based on our own ages. First person who did it gets to dare the last person or the person who's never done it. For instance, first time I ever saw a movie in a theater, I was thirteen."

"Okay, I think I get it." Oz nodded. "My parents were huge sci-fi bugs, so the first time I ever saw a movie in theaters it was probably Return of the Jedi, and I was two. But the first time I remember, I was probably four or five."

"If I didn't know better, I'd say I was set up." Graham's grumble didn't hold any weight. "That sheltered childhood I mentioned? To my parents, the kind of movies they have in theaters were anti-intellectual shit. So the first time was in college. I was eighteen."

"If it helps you feel any better, that's why it was so long for me, too." I'd snuck off to see something with my friends, when we were supposed to be back to school shopping at the mall.

"That means I win, right?" Oz looked smug. "What next?"

"Next you get to dare Graham," I said.

Oz smirked. "I like this game."

Graham rolled his eyes. "Because you're a fucking sadist."

"Not true. I don't want to see you in pain, just squirming in discomfort. Besides, I don't expect I'll win every round, and I'm not opening myself to retaliation on the first question."

"You've already formed a strategy?" I shouldn't be surprised, but I had hoped things would escalate quickly.

"I know I am," Graham said.

In that case, I needed one too. I set my brain working on the task of getting us toward fondling sooner rather than later. Within the confines of the game, of course. "Maybe I shouldn't have suggested this. I hope no one dares me to do anything too horrible."

"Fine." Graham slouched. "What do you want me to do? Streaking through the park doesn't matter, since there's no one else here."

"No streaking. I want to see that tattoo you're hiding," Oz said.

Graham had a tattoo? Wait. "How do you know that, Cole?"

"I caught a glimpse of it when he was buried to the hilt inside you."

I flushed at the memory summoned by the catch in Oz's voice.

fighting for it

"All right." Graham stood, unbuckled his belt, and undid his slacks. He tugged the waistband down his hip, exposing half a butt cheek in the process, and Celtic knot that looked like a circle woven around and through four pointed ellipses.

I brushed my fingers over the delicate ink, relishing Graham's soft skin and intoxicating groan. "What does it mean?"

"I was told it means the never-ending circle of internal strength," Graham said as he did his slacks up and sat.

"So cool." It didn't escape me that he left his belt undone. This was a good start. "Now Oz gets to go."

"First job—As in, first time someone paid you to do work for them. Fifteen. I had a paper route," Oz said.

Graham sighed heavily. "Twenty-one. TA."

I got to win a round early on. I needed a good dare, and I was pretty sure I had one. "Babysitting for the neighbors. I was twelve."

"Wait." Graham's voice brightened. "If babysitting counts, I was ten. My sister."

Oz knit his brows together. "Family doesn't count."

"Bullshit. My parents paid me, and expected me to do a good job."

As much as I wanted to hold onto my win, Graham had a point. "Oz didn't specify up front that family doesn't count. Graham wins."

Oz shook his head, but he was still smiling. "Fine. Do your worst, Graham. But remember vengeance is delayed and antagonizing."

"Pretty sure that's not how the phrase goes," Graham said.

"It is now."

Graham urged his lips and furrowed his brow. His expression stayed frozen for a moment. "Why did you leave Rinslet?"

"Don't know if you've noticed"—a hint of sarcasm lined Oz's reply—"but they're a *very* public facing company. I was sitting through my millionth meeting about how to deal with both positive and negative press, and I realized it wasn't for me. I wanted to be working with computers, not playing Bad Boy Programmer for the gossip sites."

"The man behind the curtain." I understood his nickname better now than ever.

"Exactly. Scandalous enough for you?" He looked at Graham.

"Not looking for scandal. I was curious is all."

"Your turn, Graham," I said.

"First time I kissed someone the same gender as me, I was twenty." A whisper of melancholy ghosted

fighting for it

over Graham's face. "Apparently college meant a lot of firsts."

"I think you're supposed to pick something you have a chance of winning at." A week ago, Oz probably would've said that with more disdain.

I liked that things weren't that way now.

"I think I'm supposed to pick something I want the answer to," Graham said. "Why? Are you going to come back with *ten*? Mister Bear was an early bloomer?"

"Nope." Oz *popped* on the *p*. "Same age as you. Twenty. I never let myself consider the possibility I might be attracted to men. Then one game release celebration, we were playing a game a little like this. You might be surprised to hear this, but I'm not one to back down from a dare."

Graham stared back with mock horror. "You? No."

I laughed, then shivered as a gust of chilly wind raced down my back. Clouds passed in front of the morning sun, shrouding us in shadows.

"How old, Luna?" Graham asked.

"Thirteen. Same first movie. D.E.B.S. And when I saw them falling in love on screen…" I sighed at the happy memories. "She tasted like Dr. Pepper lip gloss."

"The sexy lady is the winner." Oz boomed in an announcer voice.

"Which of us is the loser?" Graham asked.

Oz stared at him. "Don't. Make me answer that."

Graham raised an eyebrow.

I had my opening. "I get to dare you both. *Ha.* I want you to kiss."

Graham raised the second eyebrow.

Oz didn't hesitate. He captured Graham's neck, holding him captive as Oz claimed his mouth. I felt the kiss from beside them. The pressure. The intensity. The mingling of tongues and deep throaty groans.

Watching them together made my pulse race and sent need dancing over my skin. Two guys together had never been a thing for me, one way or the other, but I could masturbate to Oz and Graham doing all sorts of wicked things to each other.

Something wet struck my cheek and I swiped it away, too enthralled in seeing this kiss to give it another thought. Then another raindrop landed on my cheek. And ten more.

The skies opened up and poured buckets on us.

Kisses in the rain were incredible. Water sliding down the sharp chisel of Oz's jaw. Glistening in Graham's short beard. I was surprised the water didn't sizzle and turn to steam the moment it struck them.

fighting for it

Graham finally broke away with a groaning sigh. "We're going to freeze out here."

But it would be a happy freezing.

"That's fair." Oz released his grip on Graham's neck.

We rushed to get the cooler and wet blanket secured in the back of the truck, before sliding into the cab. *Sliding* being the operative term, given our wet butts on vinyl seats.

I looked between them—Oz's drenched and brooding versus Graham's soaked and reserved—and joy bubbled up inside, turning to laughter. "Best. Day. Ever."

My breath stalled when I met Oz's gaze again and saw the heat in his eyes. He dragged a thumb across my cheek, brushing away the rain as he traveled a path down to my mouth. He tugged my bottom lip, and dipped in to nibble on the tender skin.

I sighed against his mouth. Was Graham watching us the way I'd watched them? Geez, I hoped so. The possibility lit my senses on fire.

Oz grabbed my wrist and moved my hand to his jeans, to cup his erection. "Graham got me started for you." His voice was a rough growl against my lips.

"And I'm already wet," I teased.

"I'd fuck you right now if I thought there was room for Graham to join us without someone's legs cramping."

Graham's laugh was light. "Appreciate the consideration."

"Anything for my girl's other favorite guy," Oz said.

My girl. Not the most unique nickname, but better than the alternatives.

Graham's phone rang and he sighed. "It's Adrienne. Give me a second." He swiped *Answer.* "What's up?"

Sister calling before sex? That was a bit of a mood killer.

A tinny, indistinguishable voice drifted from his phone, and deep creases etched themselves into his forehead. "They can't do that… I'm sorry… No. I'll make it right… It is on me, it's my fault… I'll call you back when I know."

Graham dropped his phone on the dashboard with a sigh.

If I curled up next to him, would it comfort him the way it would me? "What's wrong?"

"Erol ran his complaint up to the Dean, about me being on campus and disrupting courses. She's been asked not to return."

"They can't do that." Oz stiffened behind me, and not in a sexy, *let's play* kind of way.

Graham shook his head. "No, they can't. I have to make this right for her." He raked his fingers

fighting for it

through his hair. "I have to know someone there who still has clout who can speak up for her."

"I do," Oz said. "Let me make some calls."

"I don't need you to do this for me." Like that, our morning of fun evaporated in Graham's bitter retort.

Oz sighed. "This entire thing we're working on for Luna, it's your brainchild. These are things I could never do on my own. If it makes you feel better, think of it as returning the favor."

We wouldn't be here, none of this would be happening, if it weren't for me. I was costing Oz contacts. I was damaging Graham's chances of recovering career-wise, and now Adrienne was suffering the consequences too.

Chapter Eighteen

My Thursday morning appointment was in Downtown Salt Lake, in an actual office building. The podcaster I was talking to ran several other shows as well, and was doing well enough to have an entire staff on hand.

Was I nervous?

Uh, *yeah.*

But she was friendly, greeting me shortly after I arrived and showing me around the studio. Making sure I knew where everything was, and what to expect from the show.

The *live* show.

Gulp.

But it was all right. Roxie was great about leading me through any stall-points. Filling in the dead air when I stumbled, so it wasn't obvious, and she was super friendly.

"I understand you ran into some trouble in college," she said.

No. This wasn't supposed to be part of any interview. What was she doing? My mouth was instantly dry. "I did."

"And that a member of the staff was involved."

Well, crap and double crap. I laughed nervously. "When you put it that way, it makes the entire thing sound illicit."

"Wasn't it?" Roxie's tone was kind rather than accusatory, but that didn't make me feel better about the question.

I shook my head. People wouldn't hear that. "No. Not like that."

"Like what?"

Shit. "Nothing. I don't know what I'm saying." I really didn't. How was I going to get out of this? Why wasn't I given a script? A heads-up?

"I hate that you're taking the heat for this." She still sounded nice. Concerned. "You were so young, and this older man—influential, respected—took advantage of you."

"Whoa. There was no *taking advantage*. This wasn't that kind of trouble." I could explain exactly what kind it was, but me saying *I was arrested for creating a piece of malware that threatened an entire industry. It wasn't like my teacher assaulted me* didn't seem like the right response.

Roxie's smile was sad and the way she studied me felt like pity. "I know it can be hard to admit, especially looking back on a younger you who wasn't as familiar with the world. It's easy for any of us to say now *I wouldn't let that happen to me*. But when you find yourself in that situation, at nineteen, and a person in a position of power forces their will on you—"

"I'm sorry, that's not at all what happened." I didn't want to delve into the details of my crime, but I wouldn't sit her and let her accuse Graham of things that would make him ill to even consider. "The trouble I got into was all my own doing. If you'd like, we can discuss the technical details of the code *I* created. I can decompile it for you right now." Offering to talk code should help her change the subject.

"Okay." Now she sounded condescending. How did she manage that in so few syllables? "But he got a heavier sentence than you, didn't he? What does that say about the situation?"

That my best friend's boyfriend knew people in politics and pulled some strings on my behalf. There was no way I could say that—Hunter got me this spot so Roxie knew exactly who Ramsey was. "It says I was more fortunate than he was."

Roxie finally changed the subject, but her implied accusations lingered with me through the whole hour. I gave her the most polite, sugary sweet goodbye when it was all over, and vowed to myself to never be on a show like that again.

I had to focus on keeping my hands from shaking as I waited for the bus. This was the worst kind of adrenaline rush ever, making my stomach churn and my knee bounce.

Violet called, and I almost dropped my phone trying to answer.

"I'm *so* sorry." Violet sounded as stressed as I was. "Ramsey's been on their show before, and they were always great. Hunter feels horrible. I'm so so sorry."

"It's okay." *I* wasn't okay, but this wasn't her or Hunter's fault. "They thought they were doing me a favor." But the things they implied about Graham. About my naiveté. I hated when people confused adoration with stupidity.

"I'll pick you up. We'll go for ice cream."

I smiled at her concern. "It's okay. I've got another thing tonight, and I'll use the bus ride to clear my head."

"Okay. But call me if you change your mind."

The ride home didn't do what I wanted. It wasn't the words that lingered with me so much as the implication. That I'd been too stupid to see Graham manipulating me. That this was anything other than my idea. That I was so naive I was willing to break the law for a grade. For sex? I wasn't even sure.

If I was going to be accused of doing reckless things, I wanted it to be for the right reason—because I wanted to prove I could—not because my vagina thought my teacher was pretty and I was too young and stupid to tell it *no*.

When I got home, I sifted through every piece of clothing I owned. Twice. I needed something that made me look less flighty. More mature. Smarter. Not a decade younger than the men I was dating.

The Captain Marvel dress wouldn't give me the look I wanted. Neither would the sweater with the Minnie Mouses on it.

What would Judith wear? She commanded respect just by standing in a room.

I finally landed on the same blouse I'd worn the day Oz told me he liked me. It was professional, it made my eyes bright, and it had that confidence of Oz's kisses attached to it.

I added my nicest jeans, went all out with my make-up, and pulled my hair up.

Oz and some of his people had been hired to do some higher end, last minute wiring for the exhibition we were going to. I should've taken him up on his offer to help, and skipped this morning's interview.

No going back now.

When I answered the door to Graham, he stared at me for a moment. "You look incredible."

"More than normal? Do you like this better?" I hated that my insecurities were showing through.

"There's no better or worse for you. Any way you look is another color on the rainbow of how gorgeous you are. If you answered the door in an Elmo costume, I'd be an instant furry."

His kiss was quick, but it warmed me from head to toe.

"Is this about the show earlier?" Graham asked.

And there was the memory I was trying to ignore. "Maybe."

"I'm not worried about it, and you shouldn't be either."

"But they implied—"

"And they were wrong. About you and me and every single one of their assumptions."

Hearing him back up my thoughts made me feel better. I grabbed my purse and we were on our way.

"Do you *want* me in an Elmo costume?" I asked as Graham drove. I needed to talk about anything but earlier, and that was the first ridiculous thought that flitted close.

"I want you. Full stop."

"But Elmo is super specific."

Graham moved his arm to drape over my shoulders. "Because I assume you giggle and squirm when you're tickled."

I was *super* ticklish. "Do not."

He brushed light fingers along my neck, his touch so barely there it was like a feather.

I sighed at the faint contact, until he hit a specific spot, and a squeal escaped my throat, turning to a laugh. I didn't want to break away, but the tickling became too much. "Okay. I yield. Elmo costume then?"

"No costume. But I am wishing now I'd tried that while we were back at your apartment."

I hadn't entertained that fantasy before. One where his fingers were gliding over my body until I was squirming and couldn't breathe and he was pinning me down with his full weight.

Graham was too sophisticated for something like tickling. But apparently not.

"Something to try next time," I said.

The corner of his mouth tugged up. "Definitely."

The expo was taking place in a different convention center than the auction had. Oz met us near a side entrance, away from everyone else. He gave us both a nod as we approached, and as I drew within his arm's reach, he pulled me close for a long kiss.

"Not sure which of you I'm more jealous of." Graham's teasing was gruff.

Was the other day in the park more than a one-time thing? I could handle that.

"Do you want a kiss too?" Oz asked.

Graham's cheeks darkened. "Maybe later."

fighting for it

Okay, that was super adorable that he was not only shy around Oz, but that they were actually being playful around each other.

I stepped between them, feeling ten million percent better with my hands occupied by theirs, and we headed inside. In the convention room, we were just another group of people that no one gave a second glance to.

Geez that felt good after more than a week of being everyone's focus. I was content to be at the center of my guys' world, and no one else's.

There was a stage at the far end of the room. Two long tables sat up there, holding four computers each. Giant screens hung behind them, presumably so everyone in the room could see what was being played.

There were maybe only a couple hundred people here. A huge crowd for a house party, but small for something like this.

"What is this for?" Maybe I should've asked sooner, but I hadn't been concerned with the details beyond spending the night with Oz and Graham.

"I'm sworn to secrecy," Oz said. "In fact, I didn't know until I got here this afternoon, and they only told me because I had to be on hand while they tested everything."

"Ooh." Graham dragged out the syllable. "Super Secret Secret Squirrel."

"Something like that." Oz chuckled.

"...be ashamed..."

The isolated snatch of conversation crawled up my neck.

"You guys made it." Judith joined us. She looked me over with a faint smile. "Hey. Twins."

Sure enough, our outfits could've been built from the same template. Except her trousers screamed *professional and tailored* while mine whimpered *off the rack at Walmart*, and her top was silk in a gorgeous wine color that complimented her perfectly.

Judith owned the room and I looked like a little girl playing pretend.

I pushed aside the doubt and smiled. "Apparently I've got good taste."

Graham raised my hand to lick the back. "Best taste ever."

Gross, but sweet.

"...no shame..."

"...years younger..."

I pushed out the background conversations. This morning's interview wasn't going to make me paranoid.

"We're going to start soon, but I wanted to talk to you first," Judith said. "Find me when the main event is over, because I want your opinions. Especially Luna's."

Now I was extra curious. "About what?"

"You'll see." Judith stepped away with a wave.

"*...clueless...*"

"*...pedo...*"

No. I heard that last one wrong.

"Grand denizens of industry." A booming voice flooded the room, drawing my attention to the stage. I'd met the man up there at the auction...

Dustin, that was right. He'd lost the costume and was dressed in a shirt with the same single spade on it that had been tattooed on his colleagues' arms.

"Thank you to everyone for coming out last minute." He spoke with the kind of confidence that kept everyone's attention on him. The Rinslet logo appeared on the screen behind him. "I'm sure you're all wondering what this is about. If you're not, I didn't do my job."

Light laughter rolled through the room.

"It's because tonight, we're excited to introduce AcesPlayed—because we're the first and we'll continue to be the best at what we do. Most of you know our team from our time at Rinslet—previously the most awesome gaming company in the world to work for."

The image on the large screens morphed from a Rinslet logo into the spade on his shirt, with AcesPlayed beneath it. "We're going to miss our colleagues. It's been an amicable parting of ways, but we have parted regardless."

Murmurs rolled through the crowd, and I felt the ambient curiosity and excitement in my bones.

"Tonight, we say goodbye to the people we came up in this industry with, in the most gaming way possible," Dustin said. "A little friendly competition in the game we've built. This is where you want to be recording, if you're not, because this is where I get salesy and show you something you've never seen before."

Cell phones came up, raised above heads and all pointed at Dustin. He explained this was a new kind of multiplayer RPG. It wasn't an MMO, all the servers were private, because they offered two things no one else had in this configuration.

A strictly adult only game, complete with nudity. Sex. Any sorts of hookups a person wanted, as long as it didn't break any local or federal laws. And players could either be the adventurers or the monsters.

"Ballsy," Graham muttered.

"Because Judith has bigger balls than most of the people in this room." Oz's words were nothing but respect.

Wow. I was witnessing video game history. I was here for it. I channeled my excitement into my thoughts, where chibi Luna was clapping and bouncing and squealing with anticipation.

Dustin introduced developers from each team. Rinslet would play the adventurers, and AcesPlayed were the boss monster and his add-ons.

As the teams battled back and forth, the room erupted in a wave of cheers and friendly boos. It was a close game, with dead on both sides, and stat bars in the red for anyone left standing. In the end, giant red letters flashed on the screen announcing the adventurers' party had wiped, and evil maintained its control of the valley.

Applause and boos filled the room, all good-natured.

This was abso-freakin'-lutely incredible.

Judith rejoined us as Dustin stepped forward to take questions.

"Wow." It was the first thought that came to mind. I could be more articulate than that, but for three letters, *wow* encompassed a lot.

Judith opened her mouth and someone called her name. She scowled. "Hold that thought." And she was gone again.

"So that's what innovation in gaming looks like these days." Graham sounded as impressed as me.

Oz even managed to look stunned in a good way. "It's been a long time since I've seen something like that. Pretty cool."

"...guys like that do in a game like this..."

"...in the tavern with Loli's..."

I scowled at the nearby whispers. They weren't talking about us. They couldn't be. But the words tugged at doubts and insecurities that lingered near the surface.

"...who needs to fuck cartoon little girls when he's got a real one?"

I clenched my jaw.

"Luna." Oz worked my fingers loose from the fist I hadn't realized I'd clenched them into. "Do you want to step outside?"

I shook my head and pasted on a smile. "I'm fine."

We chatted with more people Oz knew, all of them kind. Complimentary. A few even asking for my information or offering to look at my resume.

But I couldn't ignore the murmurs that grew louder the longer we were here. People quoting the show from this morning. Calling me naive. Saying Graham was a pedo-wannabe, and that I was making the same mistake with Cole.

I'd been called young and immature all my life. Whatever. But implying I was stupid. Saying horrible things about the men I was with. These gossiping assholes having no idea who the three of us were.

fighting for it

But telling myself none of the anonymous words were true didn't erase them.

The podcasts were supposed to make me look better to the public. Make it possible for me to get a job in this industry. In any industry that dealt with programming.

As the night wore on, my heart crumpled more and more, until the best I could summon to any bit of conversation was a tight smile and a brief response.

I couldn't do this. Not if it came with this kind of backlash. Not if it dragged Oz and Graham down with me, or showed them I wasn't as great as they thought.

I stuck it out as long as I could before I asked Oz to take me home. Graham walked us out to the truck.

I hugged Graham tightly and pressed my lips softly to his. "'Night." I poured everything I could into the brief exchange, swallowing my *goodbye*. I didn't want to say it now, and have them try to talk me out of it. I knew this was the right thing to do and they'd figure it out too.

Oz tried to draw me out on the ride home, but I refused to let myself be sucked into a conversation. I had him park in front of the house, rather than in the driveway. I gave him a long kiss, memorizing the way his rough hands felt on my skin as he drew the moment out.

I pulled away before I could fall into more. "'Night." I hopped from the truck and tried to keep my gait casual as I headed inside.

I pressed my back to the door and listened for the sound of Oz's truck leaving, before I let the tears spill down my cheeks. I had to end things with them, before they suffered anymore backlash from my mistake. The thought clawed under my skin and ached in my throat and my heart and everywhere.

I didn't want to, but this was the only way to give them their lives back. To give them back the anonymity and respect they deserved.

Chapter Nineteen

I wanted to sleep and let the world pass me by.

I wanted to call Oz or Graham and ask them to come get me. To keep me for the night.

I wanted to send them each a text saying things were over, so the temptation would be gone.

But if I did that now, at least one of them would show up on my doorstep. I couldn't have that while I was still here.

Instead, I spent the night staring blankly at anime I knew would make me cry. I could blame the ache in my chest on the cartoons instead of on me.

While I watched, a battle raged in my head, half of me arguing I was being stupid and the other half being logical and pointing out how Oz's and Graham's reputations had crumbled, and were continuing to deteriorate, because I was there.

As the sun came up, my eyes were raw and dry.

The cards would give me answers. They always helped me think my way through problems.

I started with my favorite deck, shuffling three times, cutting the cards, and muttering *what do I do?*

I pulled a card off the top and scowled at the reversed Two of Cups. I didn't need the freaking cards to tell me I'd just walked away from love, and it hurt like hell. I wanted to know what to do next.

This was too complex an issue to rely on a single answer.

I laid out a spread instead. When the images taunted me with more suggestions I didn't like, I resisted the urge to fling the deck across the room, and shoved all the cards back together instead.

Fine. If that deck wouldn't behave, I'd try a different one.

But the next several results weren't any better. Every fucking card mocked me with the same things the people had said yesterday on the podcast. I was being naive. Immature. I didn't know what was right for myself.

I needed Violet's help for the next step in my plan, but if I called her this morning, she'd drop everything to get over here right away. I wasn't going to disrupt another life over this.

Instead, I sent cancellation messages to the two podcasts I was supposed to be on today, with a brief *I'm sorry. I'm not feeling well.*

I hopped on a bus downtown, having long ago memorized the schedule and route that took me to the library. I loved the downtown branch, with its five stories of glass and steel.

fighting for it

Inside was sunshine and warmth and a vast stretch of knowledge. It was also quiet, since this was a midweek morning.

I made my way to their ever growing manga section, grabbed something high action that I'd been wanting to start, and settled into a bench seat by the windows.

I couldn't focus enough to read. Even my eyes hurt. How did this perfect scenario fall apart so quickly?

Because it had never been perfect. I'd ignored the consequences to live a fantasy.

As Violet's shift was coming to an end, I called her. "I'm so sorry. I need a favor." I tried to keep my voice clear, but my raw throat cracked on the words.

"Of course. What's wrong?"

I didn't want to ask this, but I was out of time and options. "I'm at the library. This is the weekend my lease is up. Can I stay in your guest bedroom for a little while? I'm looking for a place, I promise. I'll be out as soon as I can."

"You can stay as long as you need. You know that. What's wrong?"

I couldn't tell her now. I'd break down crying if I did, and then I'd also have to explain to anyone who saw me, and deal with their sympathy, and that would bounce back on me and make me feel even worse. "I'll tell you when I see you."

"Okay. I'll be right there."

A short while later, we were in Ramsey's SUV—Violet managed to get a hold of it quickly—and headed back to my soon-to-be-former apartment.

"What happened?" Violet asked.

"I'm not seeing Cole or Graham anymore."

She frowned. "What happened?" She repeated.

I didn't want to worry her, and I wasn't ready to give details about the *why*. "It wasn't working out." *Please don't ask me for details*.

Violet clenched her jaw. "You can tell me."

"I know. Soon. Not yet."

"All right."

I couldn't ignore her tone. Now I'd hurt someone else I loved. This sucked so hard.

Hunter was already at my place with his truck. Usually his easy smile and warmth brightened my day.

Today, I didn't know if anything would be ever again.

I didn't own much. My furniture all fit in Hunter's truck, and he promised to put it in storage for me. One more thing I owed someone for. My boxes went in the SUV.

When we got back to Violet, Hunter, and Ramsey's condo, it didn't take long to pack my boxes into a corner of the guest room.

Violet offered to order pizza, but I wasn't in the mood to socialize.

"We'll slide it under the door, if you prefer," Violet said. "You've gotta eat, L."

My stomach growled its agreement. "Okay. One more favor?" I had to force the words out.

"You know the answer is yes. Anything."

I did, and that made me feel even worse for asking. "If anyone asks you where I am, unless it's like law enforcement or something"—because that would be my luck—"don't tell them I'm here?"

"So *anyone* means Cole or Graham," Hunter said.

A fresh wave of doubt and pain shot through me at their names, and I nodded.

Violet scowled. She hated lying, which made this request even harder.

"Please." I spoke as plainly and emotionlessly as I could.

"All right," Violet said. She may not like it, but she'd do it. Her word meant everything.

Chapter Twenty

Graham

Watching Luna's mood deteriorate over the course of the evening was hard.

The way she said goodnight was disconcerting.

Finding out she'd cancelled her appointments today was almost as troubling as realizing she'd had Cole drop her off and ending the night at her doorstep.

Now I was staring at a text from her that had to be the briefest thing she'd ever said.

I can't see you anymore.

I replied, asking for more, and got a system message that my note couldn't be delivered. It was the same thing as I retried every thirty seconds, for the next several minutes. I paced the short span of my apartment, alternating between trying to call her and resending my text.

No answer.

I went to her apartment and hammered on the door until the upstairs neighbors told me she'd moved her things out a few hours ago, and said they'd call the cops if I didn't leave.

fighting for it

The threat didn't deter me. But if she was gone, there was no point in my being here.

Back home, I sank onto the couch and let disbelief wash over me.

What happened? I'd had Luna in my life again for such a short period of time, it couldn't be over already. She and I had what I'd never dared hope for.

Did I love her? Without a doubt. For years, but it felt more real after the last few weeks. I adored the person rather than the idea, because getting to know Luna proved daydreams couldn't hold a candle to reality.

I'd bet money she was with Violet, who I'd only met a few times when they were students. But Luna talked about her enough for me to know they were closer than sisters. Even if Luna wasn't there, Violet would know where she was.

It was inappropriate for me to either call Violet or show up on her doorstep, but it would only take me a few minutes to find her phone number or her address. It didn't matter that she was connected, I'd have the information quickly regardless.

God I was turning into a stalker.

Did that stop me from seriously considering reaching out to Violet? For about two point five seconds.

The only reason I let the possibility drift aside was because someone was ringing my doorbell. *Luna*? I couldn't help the hope that surged inside.

I peered through the peephole. *Cole.*

Not even in the same category as Luna, but not bad. I enjoyed his company far more than I expected when we met. I'd been grateful from that first day to see someone was looking out for Luna, and just as jealous of the way she looked at him.

I was happy to see him today, though.

"Where is she?" Cole asked before I finished opening the door. His demand was tinged with sadness.

I felt the sentiment on a spiritual level. I stepped away and he followed me inside, closing the door behind himself.

"You want something to drink?" I asked.

"No. I want to find Luna. You can't tell me you haven't looked yet."

How was I supposed to answer that without being insulting? Of course I'd fucking looked. But I hadn't exhausted all my options. "She's obviously hiding. Digging deeper runs a high risk of pissing her off." It was easier to tell him than to believe it myself.

Cole clenched his fist. "Seriously? This entire thing is bullshit. Don't get me wrong, I love her dearly—"

My heart caught. I knew he did, but hearing it was a different story. Cole was as much competition as he was a friend. Luna didn't see it that way, I believed her when she said that, but I hadn't moved past sentiment.

"*Fuck*." Cole sank into the same spot on the couch, in the same way that I had a short while ago, head in his hands. "I should've said that to her before you. But it's still bullshit. She's hiding for our own good, and she doesn't get to decide that any more than either of us."

"I don't have an argument."

"It took her months to find you," Cole said. "Tell me it won't take you that long to find her."

"She's with Violet." Though, now that I thought about it, Violet probably wouldn't say so, even if one of us did approach her. I know I'd lie for Luna if she asked. Without question.

Chapter Twenty-One

Cole

I'd spent my life practicing control in all things.

Luna made me want to throw it all away, and until this afternoon, I thought that was a good thing.

Graham nodded at the hand I was favoring. "Your knuckles are scuffed. What happened?"

"I punched the dashboard when I got her text." I was lucky there hadn't been anything tougher nearby. What was I doing? I couldn't pinpoint a single moment in my life when I'd reacted with this level of frustration.

But Luna was different. She was delicate enough to need to be wrapped up and shielded, but strong enough to stand alone against the storm. She'd shown me the world through a new lens. Made me believe in magic again.

"What do we do?" I didn't know if I wasn't asking Graham or myself. The only thing I was certain of, besides wanting Luna back, was this was the only place I could think of going, after I got her message.

Graham shook his head. "Not a clue. Do you want something for your hand?"

I flexed my fingers. "I'm good." If I was here, I had a friend—how did Graham become that in such a short amount of time? But I also had someone to temper my bad ideas. If I walked out the door now, I'd drive straight to Violet's, throw Luna over my shoulder, and carry her out of there.

Luna would never forgive me for that. I'd never even consider it if she were anyone else.

"I'm calling Violet." I had to do something. My phone was already in my hand, and I was scrolling through to her phone number.

"Hey, Cole." Her friendly answer was flat.

Not the kind of reception I was used to from her. "Do you know where Luna is? Can I talk to her?"

"No."

Go figure. "I asked multiple questions."

"The answer is *no*."

It was tempting to push harder. In fact, all reason insisted I do so. It wouldn't get me anywhere. "Tell her I—we—miss her. That I just want to talk."

"*If* I talk to her, I'll tell her you called," Violet said.

I'd take it. "Thank you."

"Give her a little time."

Not helpful. "I'd give her all the time in the world if I knew she was coming back." I was intently aware of Graham watching me. I'd be doing the same if our roles were reversed.

"That's not all the time in the world. It's the opposite, because you're asking her to put a timer on it." The longer Violet talked, the tighter her voice grew.

"I could make the request in person." Stupid. I shouldn't have said that. I was about to go out of my head, but the words could come across as a threat.

"Do. Not."

I bit back a growl, despite her reacting exactly the way I thought she would.

"Tell me you won't."

I clenched my jaw, reason warring with something far more primal.

"*Cole*. If you show up on my doorstep, or if you go to where Luna is, looking for her… Don't make me turn this into a threat. Respect her wishes for distance."

"Fine." I wanted to add *for tonight*. Civility beat back my inner caveman. Barely. "Thank you for looking out for her." I disconnected before I could say something stupid.

Graham scrubbed his face. He must've heard enough of the conversation to understand. "Do you want a beer or something?"

"Yeah."

fighting for it

Graham stepped around the corner, and returned with two cans of Asahai.

He handed me one, and sank into a battered easy chair as he opened the other.

I pressed the chilled aluminum to my knuckles. I was an idiotic fucking brute. "Is the Japanese beer a fanboy thing, or do you really have a taste for it?" I kept my tone light. Easy conversation might take the edge off as much as the drink.

"Both. Started off as *look at me—I'm drinking Japanese beer*. Turned out I like it." Graham took a long swallow.

Watching him, it was easy to see why Luna was physically attracted to him. He was an elegant balance of formality and fun; a walking contradiction who was fascinating to observe and talk to. It was subtle and sexy.

"First time you knew you were sunk when it came to Luna." Graham met my gaze.

"If we're playing that game, I automatically lose, because you've known her longer." Though really, we'd both lost.

Graham shook his head. "We're not playing anything. I want to know when you first looked at her and realized you couldn't walk away."

"I don't think it was a single moment." Dozens flashed through my mind as I traipsed through the last few years of knowing her. "I was doing wiring at the shelter Violet works at—upgrading the cable for internet—and this cute redhead was volunteering that day." My first thought when I'd met Luna was about how young she looked. My second, which seemed deeply irrational at the time, was *it doesn't matter as long as she's an adult.* "She was shy, but the instant we started talking tech, she opened up. By the time I realized I'd fallen for her, months later, well… I'd fallen for her."

I couldn't help my smile at the memories, despite the bitter ache in my chest. "This entire thing with Luna was one long, slow burn that flashed hot at the end, and now she's gone. It's not right."

"I know what you mean," Graham said.

"What's your moment?"

"It was my first time teaching sophomore programming, and this girl—woman? She was too young for me to be looking either way—walked in on Day One. She was wearing a green sweater as a dress, knee high socks, and Converse, and she owned it like no one's business. Even if she'd been older, while it hadn't been long since I was a student, I wasn't one anymore. It didn't matter. I couldn't take my eyes off her. She had this presence, and I had no idea how no one else noticed. And then she started challenging the lesson plan."

The easy conversation was a pleasant distraction. Focusing on how we fell for Luna? Not so much. I needed a different topic. "This idea you came up with, the planned viral concept, how did you get into teaching that?"

"I have an eye for seeing patterns in the data," Graham said. "If I pursue the research, I pick up even more, but just watching trends in different industries, I notice things. I had to know if I could reproduce what I saw, so I made it part of my thesis. When I moved into teaching, I had the support of my old teacher to try it first as a small class project, and then to put it on the curriculum."

He made it sound like a simple nothing, but he'd been teaching the kind of things most marketers would gnaw their right arm off to know.

"You could've taken that anywhere," I said. "You could be working for any of these tech giants and be at the top of the ladder."

"So could you."

"But I know why I chose not to. Why did you?" So many people didn't understand my decision. Judith was far from the only one who called me nuts for getting out of the industry.

"I already told you, I like the teaching. There's a unique level of satisfaction in showing someone how to do something, and seeing them make it their own. Watching as they grow a concept into more than it would've been if it had stayed mine alone. I like being part of that process."

Graham was so sincere with his reply. The longer he talked, the more I understood why Luna was drawn to him. My attraction ran along a different vein, but the two of them had that same thirst for discovery and sharing what they'd found.

"What did you do at Cord?" Graham asked.

I was surprised he didn't already know. "You've stalked me to the moon and back, you tell me."

"It's not stalking if I can type your name into a search engine and find it on the first page." He winced.

Because he knew he was wrong. "That's a technicality and you know it. Besides, my marriage to Judith isn't easy to find."

We didn't go out of our way to hide it, but the records weren't part of this *everything is digitized* era. And Graham had known about her from the moment he showed up on Luna's doorstep, or he wouldn't have tried to use her name to trip me up.

Graham's wince became a cringe. "All right, so there was a little bit of... stalkerish behavior. I was worried about Luna." He worked his jaw. "And jealous," he said quietly. "But I found a lot of conflicting information about your job, and I never found a solid definition of what an *Entropy Engineer* is. Is that like a game physics thing?"

fighting for it

"Not quite. My job was to adapt. If they needed Quality Assurance, I did QA. Or coding. Or site design. Or networking. I never touched art or story"—those were Jordan and Chloe's babies from Day One—"but if it was tech related, I did it."

"So cool."

The conversation drifted from there.

I stayed later than I should, and was bleary-eyed on the drive home. Graham's company numbed my frustration while I was there, but the moment I left, I was intently aware of the Luna-shaped hole inside again.

The gaping need didn't vanish overnight, and as I trudged my way through business the next day, it only got worse.

I shouldn't have promised Violet I'd stay away, which was why I found myself at their condo that evening, regardless.

Ramsey answered. Even if we'd never met, I'd know who the guy was. He had that kind of public presence.

"Can I help you?" His voice was cool.

I didn't blame him, but it wouldn't stop me. "I'd like to see Luna."

"You've got the wrong place."

"Five minutes. I don't give a fuck if you all want to listen in. Let me talk to her."

"Can't help you."

Go get her now. The command roared in my head, and I was barely conscious of drawing myself to a straight-backed posture that emphasized my height. "Please." My voice was tight, and the word came out as an order rather than a request.

Ramsey clenched his jaw and his spine went rigid.

Hunter stepped up beside him, and rested a hand on Ramsey's arm, but his attention was on me. "Leave, or I'll call the police."

Barging my way into the place and forcing Luna to talk to me wouldn't help anything, and I'd feel like an ass. The desire was still there, though. I forced myself to relax as I exhaled. "All right. I'm gone."

I'd spent years living alone, and now I was reluctant to return to an empty house. I headed for Graham's instead. It would be easy to pretend the choice was strictly because of our shared interest in Luna, but I also wanted Graham's company.

He let me in and grabbed me a soda. I shrugged off the beer this time, since I didn't need any help marring my judgment today. I settled on the couch. "I went to Violet's. It didn't go well."

Graham scoffed. "Me too. No one answered. Probably for the best."

"I held back for so long with Luna. Wanting her to have similar chances to what I had. I understand why you pushed her away *for her own good.* But telling her I was interested opened a floodgate. She pushed my inner hermit away. Somehow you do too." I didn't know where the confession came from, but it helped numb that emptiness again.

"So I'm your substitute Luna? Aren't I too old for you?" Graham teased.

I raised an eyebrow. "Touché."

Stopping by Graham's after work became an easy habit. Neither of us made the mistake of going to Violet's again, but I couldn't help leaving another message or two for Luna.

Four days in—was it wrong that I was keeping count—Violet called me.

"I get it, I do," she said. "It's not up to me to tell you if what you're doing is love or just obsession, but if Luna doesn't want it, it's stalking. Leave her alone."

Fuck.

Chapter Twenty-Two

Graham

The last thing I wanted was to give up on Luna. I'd take another three years of probation, or even jail time, if it meant seeing her again.

I was that hooked on her.

But if she wasn't interested in hearing it, I didn't see a lot of options.

For the fourth night in a row, Cole and I were sitting in my living room, making idle chatter, and pretending there wasn't a Luna-sized crater in the room.

"I'm curious about something," Cole said.

I didn't know what to make of his tone. "What's that?"

He nodded to the shelves under my TV. "Is that an original PS2?"

"It is." All of my systems were originals, but that was the one I'd played most recently so the others were tucked away.

"Favorite game?"

That was like asking a parent who their favorite child was. "There are too many to list. Last thing I played was a cart racer, and I played the fuck out of it." Which was why it was the last thing I'd played.

"A racing guy, huh?" Competition sneaked into Cole's reply. "Wanna load up a game."

I'd love to. "We can't play anything on it."

Cole's expression barely shifted, but something told me that was disbelief staring at me. "You're not going to tell me it's because that's an antique and you don't touch it?" He asked.

"Saving that answer for next time." I laughed. "But now, it's the opposite. I killed the controllers. Turns out pressing the thumb stick to the wall only makes so much of a difference, but try telling me that when I'm pushing hard for that last hidden letter, and need the perfect angle to make a jump."

"So you broke your joystick playing with it too much."

Innuendo. Nice. "Pretty much."

"I can fix it."

I smirked. Something told me I'd very much enjoy Cole playing with my joystick. "You can fix my joystick? Are you going to show me how to wiggle it the right way?"

"If a man doesn't know that by the time he's your age, there's a problem. But I can finesse it from a different angle."

I'd seen his tender side, but I'd also seen hints of roughness in the bedroom. Not that I minded either, despite my protests. "You don't strike me as a joystick finessing kind of guy."

"No? How do I strike you?"

"Let's just say I suspect it would've broken a lot sooner if you were playing with it."

"I wouldn't snap it off or anything."

My hands flew to cover my crotch. "God, I hope not. Especially if you want me to believe you're not a sadist."

Cole's laugh was a deep, throaty sound that climbed up my spine and raced down again in a delicious shudder. "Being serious for a moment," he said. "If that's the only thing keeping you from using the system, I have the tools in my truck. I can fix it."

"You know how to fix a broken game controller."

"You and Luna aren't the only geniuses around here. I'll be right back."

Cole returned a moment later with a small toolbox. He set up on the kitchen table, where the lighting was best.

It was enthralling to watch him work—big hands doing such delicate things—and he had the devices repaired in no time.

We loaded up the game and settled next to each other on the couch. It was the best way to see the TV, but I couldn't ignore the heat of his arm and thigh brushing against mine.

fighting for it

I was great at most of the games I had, and this one lingered in my muscle memory, so I won the first few races. But Cole caught on fast. By the end of the night, we were evenly matched with him winning as many games as me.

We spent the next few nights playing PS2 games and taking turns kicking each other's asses. It was ridiculous, simple, and more fun than I'd had in a while, aside from those stolen moments I'd had with Luna.

"Have you ever modded this one to play anything else?" Cole asked shortly after he arrived one evening.

I shook my head. "Not the PS2. But I've got an extra Xbox I tweaked about a billion times. It's easier to play with the OS on that."

"Wanna put a copy of Hoarde on it?"

Seriously? Duh. "What kind of geek are you?"

"Same kind as you." Cole was unfazed by my teasing question. "Is that a *yes*?"

"It's a *hell yeah, I do*."

Cole pulled a USB stick from his pocket. "Original game and source code."

I grinned. "Fucking sexy." I grabbed the device, and we hooked it up to my laptop.

We spent the rest of the night tweaking the operating system on the Xbox to support the older game.

The next night, we dove into decompiling and modding the code. But no matter what we tried, we couldn't get past the loading screen.

I was bummed when Cole had to head out at the end of the night and we didn't have the game up and running. The experience was fun, but success would've been better.

Day Three, we were spinning our wheels. Nothing we tried worked.

"We had some issues with this when we did our first builds." Cole sighed heavily. "Some of the anti-piracy security we had installed struggled on certain machines."

"If Luna were here…." I trailed off as her name tumbled past my lips. It hurt to think about her, but to bring her up made it worse. "Holy shit, I know what to do." Something she'd taught me. I made a few changes to trick the party check on load.

When we started up the game and made it to the character selection screens, I whooped loudly. Cole's *yes* was more reserved, but for him I assumed it was the equivalent of a cheer.

We fumbled our way through a level. It had been more than a decade for either of us, and games had changed a lot since this one was built, but it was a riot. We were laughing at how many times we each died, but better, it had been so much fun making this all work.

fighting for it

I looked up to see Cole watching me, heat in his gaze, and my laughter stuck in my throat.

Cole crushed his mouth to mine, and I grunted with surprise and desire. God, that felt even better than seeing it happen to someone else. He gripped the short hairs at the back of my neck, tugging and holding me captive at the same time, and deepened the kiss.

This was incredible. Not because it was physical contact and I needed to get laid, but because it was Cole. Fuck, the man could kiss.

I pressed a palm to his chest, hating that my brain had to put things on pause. "Is this… cheating?" I felt ridiculous asking, but the concern lingered.

"On whom?" Cole asked. "Our girlfriend dumped us."

"But neither of us is over her, and I know you haven't given up on getting her back any more than I have."

Oz relaxed his grip on my neck, but didn't let go. "She and I agreed to leave things open. That seeing other people was okay. In part so she could see you. I assumed the two of you talked about something similar."

"Not in so many words." Realization settled in. I'd let her assurances about the whole dating-two-guys thing make it okay, because part of me assumed I'd win her over in the end. I didn't want that now.

Not in the way that would push Cole out of the picture. "We should have."

"I wouldn't do it if I thought it would hurt either of our chances of winning her back, and I won't keep it from her once she's here again, but this is about you and me."

I was good with that. Fantastic, even. I didn't want more because it had been too long since I got laid. Cole was tugging at parts of my heart and mind Luna didn't, and together the two pieces of desire built an incredible picture.

"Okay." I leaned in and kissed him lightly.

Cole shifted his angle and leaned into the kiss, crushing against me. He dragged rough fingers over my skin, amping my desire, and I pushed back.

I couldn't get close enough. I need more contact. More skin. We stripped each other's shirts off, and it still wasn't enough. Stroking him through his jeans, the way he gripped my cock hard though my slacks in return… none of it sated the raw need that roared inside.

I'd been fighting this for too long. Focusing on Luna. She forever had a part of my heart that no one else could touch, but Cole… things had been growing between us from the day we met. Yes, the day he pinned me to the doorframe and threatened me.

This desperate gropefest was an incredible next step between Cole and me.

fighting for it

"Do you have lube?" He asked.

"Don't you? You've got everything else in your toolbox," I teased.

His glare sent goosebumps dancing over my skin. "Yes. Bedroom."

We barely let up in the kissing and teasing long enough to stumble our way into my bedroom. I was reluctant to break away, even long enough to grab the lube out of a dresser drawer.

Cole pressed into my back, his erection digging into me, and nipped along my neck. He sank his teeth into my shoulder, and I groaned loudly. God, this felt good.

He took the bottle from me. "Pants off."

"Bossy much?"

"If you expected otherwise, you haven't been paying attention."

I had, and this entire series of events pushed me beyond turned on, and had me rock hard. My cock sprung free, eager for attention, as I shed the last of my clothes.

"Kneel on the bed," Cole ordered.

I'd never been with any sort of domineering boyfriend before. I liked that Cole was my first.

He spread my ass cheeks and glided a cold slippery finger along my crack. The sharp contrast in temperature warmed quickly as he liberally applied the liquid.

Then he was nudging my entrance with the head of his cock, and sliding in one agonizing inch at a time.

It had been a while, and I'd forgotten how much I loved this feeling of being entered. Being fucked.

Cole rested inside me, occasionally twitching, but not moving much otherwise.

He reached around and gripped my dick tightly, and stroked as he started to move in my ass. He thrust in time with slow even strokes of my shaft. In and out. Up and down.

The slow build was delicious and maddening. I pushed back into Cole to increase the pace, and covered his fist with my own.

"This ends quickly if you do that," Cole warned.

"I've used up a lot of my patience over the past few years."

Cole's throaty laugh rumbled through me, and he moved both hands to grip my hips as he picked up the pace to hammer inside me.

I managed to balance myself on one arm, and stroked my own cock as he hit just the right spot with each thrust. Intensity saturated the air and I wanted to breathe it all in.

I closed my eyes as I lost myself in the combination of my touch and Cole's, and climax inched closer. Without further warning, orgasm crashed around me, sending a shower of stars to dance behind my eyelids. I came hard, coating my hand, thrusting against my grip until my skin was too tender and slippery for any more.

Cole reached climax quickly after I did. Grunting. Pounding. Slowing to a stop. He kissed up my spine, pulling me upright as he moved higher and his dick slipped out of me. "Fuck." His simple statement rolled over me.

I didn't have a better word for it.

"Mess on the blanket," he said.

Great. I was the cause of the wet spot. "I have others."

We washed up, changed the comforter out, and collapsed naked together on the bed.

"I need to find a way to fall asleep with the two of you at my place," Cole said. "You've got some crummy mattresses."

I smiled and pressed closer into him. "Now you're a bed snob?"

"Yes."

"*And* you assume that *the two of us* are still an option."

"I need Luna back." Cole's conviction rumbled through me. "Tell me you don't."

"I do. Desperately." We had to figure out how to get her to hear us out.

Chapter Twenty-Three

Luna

I spent days walking up and down streets in different parts of different cities in the valley, applying for any job where there was a help wanted sign. I'd done this before, and it had never panned out, but I had to try again.

I missed Oz and Graham so much the ache overrode my sore feet and tired legs.

Violet had told me when Cole stopped by, and that he and Graham both called. They'd called me, too. The calls stopped when she threatened them. I was grateful I hadn't had to tell them myself to stop, because I would've cracked.

If that happened, if I went back to them, their lives would fall apart again. Their names and mine had vanished quickly from current media once I walked away.

Both men filled my nights in the form of dreams, but that was the case before, too. The longing was more potent than before I'd had a taste, but at least I had reality to flavor the fantasies now.

fighting for it

I wanted to lose track of the days to let time wash around me and make me forget what I'd had. I knew exactly how long it had been since I saw Oz and Graham, though. Thirteen days, twenty hours. If pressed, I could recite the minutes and seconds, too.

I was sitting on the bed, pretending I could focus on the book on my phone, when Violet knocked on the bedroom door.

She joined me without waiting for a reply, sitting next to me, back to the headboard, and knees propped up. "Why are you doing this?" She asked. "You're miserable."

"I have to. It's the only way." I thought Violet of all people would get it without me having to explain. "You almost left Ramsey because of the public attention."

"No. I almost left Ramsey because he was asking me to lie about who we were. You know the difference between that and bad press."

My insides twinged. I wanted comfort, not to be called out. "This isn't just bad press. It was ruining their lives. Oz's colleagues, the things they were saying about him. And Graham… he was already struggling to find work, and he loves teaching." I took that from him, and I didn't know how to give it back.

"So first of all, since when do you care what other people think, and just as important, they're adults. They can make their own decisions about what does and doesn't ruin their lives. They've survived this long."

I searched for words, but the only thing I found was *how dare you,* and I couldn't summon the indignation to go with the retort.

"Well?" Violet asked.

You're supposed to back me up. You're supposed to be my friend. "If you're worried about them calling or coming by again, I'll find somewhere else to go. I can get out of your hair."

Violet sighed and leaned her head against mine. "You know that's not what this is about. Why are you really here? Why are you really avoiding them?"

"I already told you." I pulled away in frustration and stood.

But her question reached inside and grabbed thoughts I'd been successfully shoving aside, and I pushed back on my own insecurities.

"L. I'm worried about you. I love you. I don't want to see you hurting, especially not yourself." Violet pushed to her feet as well. "I don't think I've ever seen you like this. Even after you were arrested. Even after you were sentenced. Something more is going on. Why did you walk away from Cole and Graham?"

fighting for it

"Because I'm a silly little girl who's really good at letting my curiosity fuck things up, and they deserve better." The confession tumbled out on a gasp of despair and I squeezed my eyes shut. I hadn't meant to say that out loud. I hadn't even let myself think that full thought.

"You're an adult ass woman, as much as they're adult men. You're not fucking up anyone's lives, and that's their decision, not yours. Did you even tell them *goodbye*?"

I ducked my head and hugged myself. If I stopped answering, would Violet leave me alone? Not that I wanted her gone. I couldn't lose her, too. What was I doing? The confusion hit me full force.

Violet wrapped me in a tight hug, squeezing before letting go. "You know my commute between the shelter and Loading Java takes me past Graham's."

No it didn't. "Not without doubling your travel time."

"Cole's truck has been out there the couple of times I've driven past."

"Your point is?" My chest was threatening to collapse in on itself.

"Why are you hiding from them?"

"I told you why."

Violet clucked. "That's not a good reason. If someone told you the same thing, you'd be furious."

I had been. When Graham said it, it was enough to push me away. I should've—

My mind refused to finish putting words to the thought. "You know what makes me furious?" Speaking was better than falling into my head. "Doing podcast after podcast, for days on end. Applying for job after job, and not getting a call back, even though I'm the fucking best at what I do. Because why? Because I've got a record? Because I'm a girl? Because I'm a girl with a record?"

Now that the words were flowing, I couldn't stop them. "And Graham and Oz have expectations. Of me. They think I'm going somewhere. They've both told me this. They think that because I have this talent, that I'm going to do great things with it." I gasped at my own confession. "What if I'm not that person?" It hurt to say. I'd never vocalized that fear, even to myself, and it tied a knot in my heart to admit it. Despair bubbled up inside and a sob tried to work its way out. "There's nothing wrong with me waiting tables. Or working a cash register. Sweeping floors. I don't have to be great to make a difference."

"It's true." Violet's voice softened. "But those aren't the things you want to be doing."

"I wouldn't mind."

She tugged my arms apart and grasped my fingers. "Are you worried about letting the guys down, or are you worried about seeing your expectations for yourself reflected back at you, when you look at Cole and Graham?"

"That doesn't make any sense." But it did. If I pushed them away, I could say my success was their dream.

"Doesn't it? Come here." Violet led me into the guest bathroom and pointed me at the mirror. "What do you see?"

I didn't want to look at my reflection. Not figuratively or literally.

"Humor me." Violet gently forced my gaze up.

Sad green eyes stared back at me. Heavy shadows under pale skin were obvious underneath. I still wore the makeup I'd put on to fill out applications. Was still in the generic blouse and trousers, with my hair pulled back.

"What do you see?" Violet asked.

"I don't know. Me?"

"Are you sure?"

No. The person in the mirror was like pod person Luna. Made up to blend into the world, rather than explore her way through places most people never noticed. I turned away, stalked back to the bedroom and flopped on the bed.

Violet lingered in the bathroom doorway. "For as long as I've known you, you've had this drive to learn and to use that knowledge. To dissect the universe, figure out what makes it tick, and tweak until it ticks better. You've never been satisfied with the status quo. I know this has been hard on you. The arrest. The probation. The publicity."

"Are you going somewhere with this?"

"But you pulled through it all. You stayed true to you. Now that you've pushed Graham and Cole away, you've given yourself a reason to give up. To hate yourself, when you've never surrendered before."

"I don't—" My voice cracked.

"This is going to get better. The media. The trouble finding work. You will achieve great things, even though you're stumbling now. Not because someone else expects you to, but because that's who you are, L."

I rolled over on my side and pulled the blanket over me. "I'm going to sleep."

"It's five in the evening."

"It's a nap."

Violet yanked the covers off me. "Go take a shower. Put on some of *your* clothes. Not whatever you think will impress some small business, but something that you own that makes you smile. And then I'm taking you to Graham's."

I was tempted. Everything Violet said hurt. Pissed me off. Made me admit things to myself I didn't want to. She was also right.

fighting for it

"I'm scared." Another confession, but this one didn't hurt as much. "What if things stay hard?"

"They won't be forever. And they'll be a lot easier if you stop pushing people out of your life who you love. Who love you."

Chapter Twenty-Four

In a way I was reluctant to admit Violet's kind version of tough love was working. But having my hair hanging loose and damp, knowing I didn't have to tame the messy waves that would dry, was oddly comforting. And this time I was wearing the Captain Marvel dress, with my old, battered pair of Vans.

This time the Luna who stared back at me in the mirror was almost smiling. Which made me smile more. Which made a big ball of warm sunshine spread through me.

Until I remembered how badly I'd screwed things up with Graham and Oz. And I still didn't know if Violet was right about going back to them.

Anxiety bubbled up inside as Violet drove me to Graham's. Sure enough, when we arrived, Oz's truck was parked out front.

Violet pulled me into a tight hug. "Call me if you need anything," she said. "You're brilliant, you're sexy, and you're going to be all right."

If I let the happy tears squeeze out, my eyeliner would smudge. It didn't matter how nervous I was, I still hoped the ruined makeup wouldn't happen until Oz was having his way with me.

"Thank you." I squeezed back, stepped from the car, and forced one foot in front of the other until I was in front of Graham's door.

As I knocked, I flashed back to just a few weeks ago, when I stood her for the first time with Cole, hoping above hope that Graham would want to see me.

Even the way he opened the door and stared at me was too much like last time. Except today, Oz was standing next to him, not me.

Silence stretched between us. It was only a second or two, but it felt like an eternity. My words stuck in my throat.

Graham placed a finger under my chin, tilted my head up, and kissed me hard. Hungrily. Devouring my gasp of surprise and my repeated *I'm sorry.*

"It's fine." He nipped at my lips. "As long as you're here now. As long as you're not leaving again." He pulled me into his apartment, still kissing me over and over, and the door closed behind us.

Hands rested on my hips and Oz spun me to face him. He lifted me as he crushed his mouth to mine, pressing my back to the door. I had to wrap my legs around his waist and my arms around his waist to hold on.

If he leaned into me any harder, we might melt together and become one. I was fine with that. I wanted to stay wrapped up here with him, with Graham, forever. All my reasons for leaving lay whimpering and useless by the side of my mind.

I could move into this feeling of warmth and belonging, start a little commune, and build a happy ranch of rainbows and sexy brilliant men. Two specifically.

Oz spun with me still wrapped around him, his hands on my ass holding me to him, and walked us into the bedroom to deposit me on the bed. He knelt at my feet, never breaking the kiss for more than a heartbeat.

Graham was behind me, lips gliding over my neck and fingers dancing up my sides.

"Should we talk?" I finally found enough of a pause to speak. Not that I didn't want this—I wanted it more than almost anything—but I couldn't ignore that the last few weeks happened.

"Does talking involve any form of you leaving?" Oz asked.

Now that I was here, I couldn't imagine being without either of them again. "I'm here to stay. I mean, not specifically. I'm not movi—"

Oz silenced me with another kiss.

"But yes, I suppose we should talk." Graham's words hummed against my shoulder.

fighting for it

Oz groaned into my mouth and broke away. "You know we're in this relationship with you because we want to be. Because we want you. Because we believe in you."

That last bit yanked on my insecurities again, because I did know that. "*We*? You speak for Graham now?"

"For this he does," Graham said.

"What if I can't live up to your expectations?" Or my own.

Graham wrapped his arms around my waist and pressed into my back. "This isn't about expectations. It's about hope and possibility and being happy. Don't let a couple of missed steps take your spark away"

The sentiment was sweet and painful and wonderful.

"You're like a unicorn." The adoration in Oz's voice made my heart catch. "You're magical, mystical, and the kind of elusive magic people spend their lives chasing, but never find."

I didn't know how to respond. "Are you going to name me *Horny*?"

Oz's smile was half amusement and half feral and completely delicious. "No. I'm going to call you Luna. *My* Luna. Every night that you've been gone I considered kicking down Violet's door to get you."

"She would've killed you." I was horrified by the idea, and that any part of me thought it was a sweet sentiment.

"You wouldn't have forgiven me, and that was what held me back. I've never been that guy before, but you make me surrender all reason. I love you, Luna."

My heart swelled in my chest. "I love you too. So much." The longer I sat here, pressed between them, the lighter I felt. It'd be neat if we just kind of floated away in a cloud of bliss.

"Feeling a little left out here," Graham said lightly.

I leaned more of my weight into him and pulled his arms tighter around me. "You're as much a part of this equation for me as Oz is. I'm sorry I ruined your life."

"Don't." Graham was stern. "It's like you keep saying, I made my own decisions. Some of them were for the challenge, a lot more of them were so I could spend time with you, but all of them brought us to this point. My life isn't ruined. There were downs, there were some amazing ups and there will be more. My world shines brighter with you in it. You're my heart. My mind. My sanity. And I was an idiot to push you away. I need you here with me. With us. I don't care what comes next as long as we're all facing it together."

fighting for it

My heart was soaring. Both Graham and Oz's repeated use of *we* and *us* to describe them both didn't escape me either. That must be quite a story. I felt their love and hope and both spoke to something I'd been missing since I cut myself off from them.

And then Oz was kissing me again. So was Graham. Mouths gliding along my neck, my lips, my jaw, my ears, my shoulders. Most if their attention stayed above my neck except for the occasional hand that glided up my side or over my stomach.

It was about as chaste as being pinned between two men could be.

"What do you want, right at this moment?" Oz asked. "Anything."

Double banana split with extra fudge probably wasn't the kind of mood-enhancing answer he was looking for. It wasn't what I wanted anyway. I wanted that first night with Oz, but times two. I bit my bottom lip.

Oz's wicked smile was back. "Tell me."

"Use me like a set of holes. Fuck me hard and fill me up until I'm sore and sticky."

Graham's groan rumbled against my back. "How is that a turn on when you say it?"

"Because you're as filthy and desperate as she is," Oz said. "And I'm gonna let you watch. If you're lucky, I'll let you have a taste." He shifted me on the mattress enough to pull me from Graham and push me roughly onto my back, pinning me in place with his hand on my stomach.

Graham grabbed my wrists. He was more gentle than Oz had been doing the same thing, but I still couldn't break free. Not that I wanted to.

Oz forced his knee between my legs, pressing it against my pussy, prompting me to grind against him. He shoved my dress to my chest, and kneaded my breasts hard enough to draw a long groan from me.

Each new pinch, twist, and light slap from Oz had me whimpering louder. Squirming. Loving every minute of it as I fell into bliss.

Oz removed his knee to push the crotch of my panties aside and penetrate me with his fingers. Without the fabric, my thighs were coated in an instant as he fingerfucked me and abused my nipples.

I was lost enough in pleasure that I was barely aware of him removing one hand. I heard the sound of tearing foil. He slid his fingers from me, and my body groaned at the sudden absence of any sensation besides Graham pinning me in place.

I hoped he was fucking enjoying the show. I was certainly enjoying being part of it.

Oz thrust his cock inside me without warning, burying himself deep and stretching me out. I'd missed this far more than was reasonable considering it had only been a few weeks.

fighting for it

I rocked against him as he glided in and out, over and over, enough to work me to the brink of anticipation. I knew how this part of the game worked. If I wanted more, I'd have to beg, and I may or may not get it right away. The odds were part of the fun.

"Make me come, please?" I whimpered.

"No." Oz pulled out again. "In fact, if you touch yourself, no orgasms."

Geez, this was the most delicious torture.

Oz moved to kneel next to me instead, reached past me, and grabbed Graham by the back of the neck. Graham obeyed the silent prompting, crawling forward to draw Oz into his mouth, licking my juices away.

H. O. T.

Oz forced Graham's head up. "You can have Luna next," Oz said. "If you can make me come."

Wowza. I squeezed my thighs together to try to fight the throb. My fingers itched to slide between my legs. To stroke myself while I watched Graham on his knees in front of Oz.

I rolled up onto one elbow, partly to get a better view, but just as much to make it easier to resist the need pulsing under my skin.

The groans that filled the room drove me wild. The pleasure on both of their faces. The way

Graham's cock hung hard and eager between his legs. The way Oz slammed against his face.

Oz's grunts said he was close. He let out a long sighing shudder, and stopped.

The way Graham looked up at him, eyes wide, chin wet, as if he needed permission, clenched around my chest and made me want to be a part of that sandwich.

Tilting Graham's head, Oz gave him a soft kiss. "She's all yours."

Graham rolled a condom on, scooted my butt toward him, and knelt between my legs. The heat and glazed look on his face probably reflected my own.

The way he slid inside me was both a relief, and not nearly enough to sate my roaring desperation.

Oz moved closer, dragging a thumb over my bottom lip. "My gorgeous little cock slut. Does he feel different than me?"

"Yes. Longer, but not thicker. He can still make me come hard, though."

Oz lowered himself to brush his lips over mine. "He'd better." He lowered his mouth to one nipple, and I arched into his mouth when he scraped his teeth over the tender skin before sucking hard.

Graham pounded inside me with reckless abandon, slamming harder and faster. From the sounds he was making, he wouldn't last long.

Oz dipped his fingers between my legs, stroking my clit, teasing me, easing off every time my breathing grew shorter.

When Graham reached that point where he was all fast grunts, Oz pushed me harder, drawing me into the longest, most delicious climax. I clenched around Graham, milking him as he came. Squeezing tight and savoring every inch of him deep inside me.

The rest of the world didn't exist as we slowed to a stop. The only thing here were my guys. Sweet. Protective. Utterly fuckable.

Oz cleaned me up, and Graham stayed curled around me while Oz changed out the comforter. Apparently that big wet spot was my fault. I didn't have the brainpower to ask when Oz had become so comfortable changing the bedding in Graham's apartment.

We all squeezed into the bed, and Oz pulled me into him.

Graham pressed into my back, trailing his fingers through my hair. "God, you're so stunning."

"Hmm." Oz's grunt rumbled through my cheek. "Indeed."

I ran my fingers through the fine hairs on Oz's chest, memorizing every sensation. His warmth. The tickles of his chest fuzz. The beat of his heart against my cheek and Graham's against my back. I could sink into this for a long, long time.

Chapter Twenty-Five

I dozed, wrapped up my in my men and feeling safe. Each time I managed to register the clock, thirty minutes had passed, or sixty. The sun had set and the sky was growing dark. It was almost nine.

I forced myself to consciousness again when Oz extracted himself to answer a ringing phone. He came back into the room a moment later. "Call for..." He put the receiver back to his ear. "How did you phrase it?" He listened for a moment before holding the device toward me. "Call for the adorable little sprite who holds my leash."

"*Sprite* doesn't work for me," Graham said. "It's too much like Soda. *Imp*?"

I scrunched up my face. "No. Game of Thrones call backs."

Oz looked at us, brows raised. "Would you like to take this, or should I tell her to call back?"

"Her?" My curiosity swelled and I took the phone. "Hello?"

"You're a hard woman to get a hold of." It was Judith.

Calling for me? "I've been screening my calls."

"Never screen me again."

"Yes, ma'am." The agreement slipped out before I could consider the words.

"Damn straight." Her tone lightened. "I know it's late, but is now a good time?"

"For...?"

"A job interview."

What in the what? Did I even remember how to act in an interview? Was there a different protocol when it was with my boyfriend's ex-wife? Who also happened to own what was about to be the hottest game on the market. "Of course."

"What did you think of the game?" Judith asked.

In order to tell her, I'd have to separate the bad of that night from the good. Doing so would be a lot harder if I didn't have Graham next to me and Oz climbing into bed again. Was it weird to do a job interview naked? Was it irony, considering the kind of game Judith was making?

I pulled the sheet tighter around me, like it would make any difference in the grand scheme of things. "I love the idea. The gameplay looks incredible. The concept is top notch. It's been a long time since I saw something so innovative, and honestly I'm a little jealous of the people who get to work on it." But she'd said job interview. I didn't want to let my hope skip ahead several steps, but it was too late.

"A game like ours needs airtight security," Judith said. "Not just to keep the bots out, but to make sure minors can't get in. To ensure privacy. Protocols have to be top notch and impenetrable."

"No offense, but there's no such thing."

"If you were going to keep yourself out, how would you do it?"

The pieces slid into place in my mind in an instant. Age verification. Layers of checking. Firewalls. Encryption. Salt. Hashes.

I reeled off about three sentences before Judith said, "Hold up. Wow, you make me feel out of the loop, and I own the fucking company."

"Security development is a different mindset than game development." I had respect for both, and she could without a doubt teach me a few things about her side of the business.

"It is," Judith said. "I had to let one of our security developers go two weeks ago. A company like ours has to be twice as vigilant about things like harassment and privacy violations, and the lawyers won't let me say more beyond *he wasn't working out.*"

"I'm sorry to hear it."

fighting for it

"I'm glad we caught it before it became more of an issue. Would you like to come work for me? On the hottest *coming soon* game in the industry?"

I hoped the offer was coming the moment she said *job interview*, but I still needed to process the word. "I'm sorry. What?"

"You heard me. You don't have to answer tonight, though. Text me your email, and I'll get you a contract so you can think things over."

"That won't be necessary." Crap. That might sound like I was turning her down. "I mean, yes. I want the job. *Yes.*" My excitement bubbled to overflowing. "I definitely want it. Yes over and over. When can I start?"

Judith laughed. "Are you sure?" She was lightly sarcastic. "How does Monday sound?"

"Brilliant. I love it. I'll be there. Thank you, thank you!" I disconnected and handed Oz his phone before I realized I hadn't gotten details. Office location. Dress code. Working hours. My mind was racing so fast it could barely keep up with itself, I was so excited.

Oz's phone buzzed, and he showed me the text from Judith with all the information and an *I'm looking forward to it.*

"*Yay.*" I clapped and bounced.

"I assume *congratulations* are in order?" Graham looked amused.

I should stop bouncing. I couldn't. I gave him a huge hug and kiss, and then one for Oz. "Do you know how amazing this is?" The question was rhetorical. Everyone must know.

"Should we be hurt that seeing us again didn't earn that kind of response?" Graham asked.

Seriously? There was no contest. "Do you want me to beg Judith to call me a filthy whore and plead for her to fuck me?"

"Definitely not," Oz said quickly. He pressed a long kiss to my lips, drawing out my breath and making my heart skip. "Congratulations."

This was so incredible. This was I couldn't have imagined a more perfect fantasy level of wonderful. The job was the cherry on top of the banana split sundae. Being caught between Oz and Graham, feeling the warmth in the room, the love, was the best thing ever.

It set a high bar for what came next.

And I had no doubt we'd beat that benchmark over and over.

Epilogue One

One Month Later
Graham

Luna spent weekdays at my place, with Cole stopping by after work more often than not, despite the cramped quarters with three of us here. It made getting Luna to work easier, but mostly it was because we all wanted to spend that time together.

Cole offered to buy Luna a car, and she made him promise not to. She was making more with this job than she knew want to do with, and a car was one of the first things on her to-buy list. She did agree to let Cole co-sign for her, though.

On weekends, all three of us spent our time at Cole's in Jeremy Ranch. We all had keys to both places. The entire thing became routine quickly, and I adored it.

I was still doing tutoring. That hadn't picked up, but I enjoyed the work, so I wasn't complaining. I was at the tail end of a video tutoring session when I heard my apartment door unlock.

The *Recording in Progress* sign on the front door would tell whoever it was that I was working, but the others were supposed to both be at their own jobs still.

Cole poked his head around the corner of the kitchen, where I sat at the table. I gave him a slight nod, but kept my attention on the lesson and my student's last minute questions. He settled on the couch, which I could see from my seat, and scrolled through his phone.

I wrapped up class about ten minutes later, and took the spot next to him. "You're here early."

"I wanted to watch you work." Cole rested a hand on my knee. He liked the contact with either Luna or I, and I certainly wasn't complaining.

I didn't know what to do with his statement, though. I still had a hard time telling when he was being serious and when he was joking. I got it right more often, but right now he sounded serious, and there was no way he could be. "Your own work was that dull?" I teased.

"It was that busy. I need to bring on a couple more internship supervisors."

"Very cool. Congrats." It made me happy to hear that things were going well for Cole, on several levels.

"So when can you start?" He asked.

"I—" I laughed. "What?"

fighting for it

"You heard me."

I had a brief flashback to the night Luna was offered a job. I flashed back a lot to that night, but usually the sex and *I love yous* that came before that moment. "You want me—"

"Frequently. But to finish the thought, yes, I want you to come work for me."

What was I missing? "I thought you didn't fuck people involved with the job." I'd heard the story about how Cole kept his distance from Luna for so long, and while I could imagine the kind of restraint that took, I also didn't understand why Cole made that choice. He was the boss. He didn't have to place those restrictions on himself.

"I said *with* me, not *for* me. Do you really think this is just fucking?"

"No." Not to me it wasn't.

Cole sighed. "When Luna was in my program, I told myself I wasn't making a move for her because she worked for me. It was an excuse. I wasn't doing it because… I didn't want to be the dirty old man corrupting her."

I knew this story all too well. "Everything you accused me of."

"We frequently accuse others of our own worst flaws."

"That's poetic."

He trailed his thumb along the seam of my jeans in a lazy path. "She's more to me than *a fuck*, obviously, and so are you. I want you in my life, in our lives. I need another person who can do both administration and training at the office, and I've never met anyone more qualified than you. I don't care if you keep tutoring. You can set your own hours with me."

I was more of a nine-to-five kind of guy than a pick-my-own-schedule dude. Was it wrong that the idea of set hours was kind of a turn-on? And being a part of what Cole did… "Yes. I'd love to sign on."

"Welcome aboard, partner." The way he said *partner* heated my blood.

The way he pressed his lips to mine raised my temperature to scorching. God, I loved kissing this man.

The door clicked open again, interrupting the moment.

"You didn't wait for me?" Luna's voice was playful as she stepped into the apartment.

We had a *we don't all have to be there for sex* agreement that was working out great, so I wasn't worried about hurt feelings or jealousy. When we first discussed it, I thought it would be hard to adjust, but I couldn't imagine doing things any other way.

"I saved some things for you," Cole said.

fighting for it

"Oh my head." Luna pressed her palms to her cheeks in a perfect *Home Alone* impersonation. "There's more than watching the two of you kiss?" She crossed the room to join us.

We each grabbed a wrist and tugged her to sit across our laps. She winced and shifted her shoulder, but her smile returned so quickly I could've imagined it left at all.

"Not that I mind," I said. "But how did I get lucky enough to have both of you here at three on a weekday afternoon?" I was supposed to pick Luna up from work, so her arriving alone was a double surprise.

"Boss gave me the afternoon off to recover." Luna's tone was cheerful.

Cole frowned. "Recover from what?"

I shared his concern.

Luna pulled up her shirt sleeve to reveal a spade tattoo covered in plastic. A lot of the people at AcesPlayed had them.

My concern climbed higher at seeing the fresh ink. "You know that's—"

She silenced me with a look. "Permanent? Yes. I'm aware. You weren't going to question whether or not I thought about this, were you?"

I was, but not now.

"It's a good point." Cole didn't seem to have the same reservations.

Luna grinned. "Yeah, the job may not work out—not that I'm worried—but even if for some ungodly reason it doesn't, I still want a reminder that I was part of it. Of this new, incredible piece of technology."

"Did it hurt?" I asked. Mine hadn't been bad, but one never knew.

"Like you wouldn't believe. I want to get another one in a few months."

Cole nuzzled her neck. "My sexy little pain slut."

God, I loved everything about this. Cole. Luna. Our time together. The blend of brains, personalities, and fun…

I couldn't imagine a better future than one with the two of them in it. I never would've dreamed this up to begin with, it was so implausible and wonderful. I couldn't wait to see what came next, as long as it involved all of us.

Epilogue Two

Cole

"What was this about saving something for me?" Luna asked.

Graham nodded toward the kitchen. "There's a piece of chocolate cake in the fridge. The kind with extra frosting that only you like."

Luna clapped with glee. *Fuck* that was adorable.

"But that's from you, not Oz," she said.

"True."

I was stalling. Which was stupid, since I hadn't hesitated about anything this way in a long time. Not since Judith. On second thought, I don't think even that meant this much to me.

"Are you nervous?" Graham asked in disbelief.

I stared back. "Fuck you." My tone was light.

He grinned. "Not until after you tell us. Distracting me with offers of sex doesn't get you off the hook."

"The commutes are getting to be a bit much." Best I get it over with, or he'd make a big deal out of things, and then Luna would join in… That would be fun, but it would delay what I really wanted.

"I get paid in a week, and it'll be enough for a down payment on a car." Luna's voice was meek.

I smiled. I was so excited to see her doing this. "Not what I meant. I don't mind chauffeuring you around. What I mind is leaving either of you at the end of the night. Also, sleeping in Graham's bed. I mind that lumpy piece of shit a lot."

"Fucking hell, really?" Graham's sigh was exaggerated.

Double adorable. "One of my rental homes just opened up. I'm doing a lot of work down here in the valley, you're both situated here, and I was wondering if I should take the rental off the market so we can make it our second home."

"I think I need a first home in order to have a second."

"The place up in Jeremy Ranch is the first," I said. "You know, that tiny little chateau where we spend our weekends?"

Graham scoffed. "Tiny. Pft."

"Wait…" The pieces clicking in Luna's head were almost audible.

"You're getting it."

She stuck her tongue out at me. "You're suggesting we all move in together."

"I'm *asking* that we make it official." I may control her in the bedroom, but I would never presume to order her around day to day.

Her grin brightened the room. "My cards said it was going to be an amazing day. I thought they meant the tattoos, but—"

"Is that a yes?" I didn't mean to cut her off. I was more anxious than I should be for an answer.

"Can I bring the bed?" Graham asked.

I fixed him with a glare. "No."

"I guess I'm in anyway." He sighed heavily.

Luna elbowed him lightly. "You can't see, but I'm cheering in my head. Full-blown chibi me, complete with pom poms. Yes. Yes, A million bazillion times, *yes*."

"Fuck, I love you." I brushed my lips over hers. I turned to Graham, holding his gaze. "And you. I love you so very deeply." It was the first time I'd said that, and it felt incredible.

Graham's breath caught as he stared back. "I love you too. God, you irritate the hell out of me sometimes, but I love you immensely. I can't imagine a future that you're not a part of. Both of you."

As I kissed him, and Luna, and Graham again, I couldn't help but think this was perfect. Better than perfect. This was the ultimate in amazing, and it was ours.

———

About Allyson Lindt

USA Today Bestselling Author Allyson Lindt is a full-time geek and a fuller-time author. She's found her own happily ever after, where she and her spouse call their furbabies their children. Coffee is her task-master and random tangents are her muse. When she's not writing, she's fangirling over the latest superhero movies. She likes her stories with sweet geekiness and heavy spice, and loves a sexy happily-ever-after. Because cubicle dwellers need love too. Learn more about Allyson's books, including signing up for her newsletter, by visiting http://www.allysonlindt.com.